Done

EMERGENCE

THE REDEMPTION TRILOGY

AJ SIKES

GREAT WAVE INK
PUBLISHING

GREAT WAVE INK
P U B L I S H I N G

Cover Design by Elizabeth Mackey
ElizabethMackeyGraphics.com

GREAT WAVE INK
P U B L I S H I N G

This book is dedicated to the FDNY, and to the VFD in Vacaville, California. A portion of the author's proceeds from sales will be donated to the FDNY Foundation and the VFD Victims Assistance Fund.

Foreword
by
Nicholas Sansbury Smith

Dear Reader,

Thank you for picking up a copy of Emergence by AJ
Sikes. This is the first of the Redemption trilogy
documenting the lives of several main characters from the
Extinction Cycle main storyline, including New York
firefighter Meg Pratt.

Originally published through Amazon's Extinction
Cycle Kindle World, Emergence became a reader
favourite in the Extinction Cycle series side stories, and
transcended to far more than fan fiction. Unfortunately,
Amazon ended the Kindle Worlds program in July of
2018 with little warning. Authors were given a chance to
republish or retire their stories, and I jumped at the
chance to republish Emergence through my small press,
Great Wave Ink. Today, we're proud to offer Emergence
in paperback, audio, and to readers outside of the United
States for the first time ever.

For those of you that are new to the Extinction Cycle
storyline, the series is the award winning, Amazon top-
rated, and half a million copy best-selling seven book
saga. There are over six *thousand* five-star reviews on
Amazon alone. Critics have called it, "World War Z and
The Walking Dead meets the Hot Zone." Publishers
weekly added, "Smith has realized that the way to rekindle
interest in zombie apocalypse fiction is to make it louder,

longer, and bloodier… Smith intensifies the disaster efficiently as the pages flip by, and readers who enjoy juicy blood-and-guts action will find a lot of it here."

In creating the Extinction Cycle, my goal was to use authentic military action and real science to take the zombie and post-apocalyptic genres in an exciting new direction. Forget everything you know about zombies. In the Extinction Cycle, they aren't created by black magic or other supernatural means. The ones found in the Extinction Cycle are created by a military bio-weapon called VX-99, first used in Vietnam. The chemicals reactivate the proteins encoded by the genes that separate humans from wild animals—in other words, the experiment turned men into monsters. For the first time, zombies are explained using real science—science so real there is every possibility of something like the Extinction Cycle actually happening. But these creatures aren't the unthinking, slow-minded, shuffling monsters we've all come to know in other shows, books, and movies. These "variants" are more monster than human. Through the series, the variants become the hunters as they evolve from the epigenetic changes. Scrambling to find a cure and defeat the monsters, humanity is brought to the brink of extinction.

We hope you enjoy Emergence and continue on with the rest of the Redemption series, and the main storyline in the Extinction Cycle. Thank you for reading!

Best wishes,
Nicholas Sansbury Smith,
USA Today Bestselling Author of the Extinction Cycle

— 1 —

April 19ᵗʰ, 2015
South Jamaica, Queens

Meg Pratt went through her bathroom rituals and got dressed as fast as she could, taking care not to strain anything. The run that morning had been a real challenge. She had to change her pace a lot and dodge more cars than usual, even a few moving vans. It was a weird time of year for people to move out, she'd thought.

The cat was curled up on her dresser and gave a little *mewl* when she scratched behind his ears.

"We'll have a nap later, Biggins."

The cat gave her a narrow-eyed stare before he tucked his face back down into his paws. Meg gave the cat a pretend *Harrumph* and went to join her husband, Tim, for breakfast.

In the kitchen, Meg poured her coffee and sat down at the breakfast counter while Tim whipped up an egg white omelet for them to split. Behind Meg, the spring time skies of New York City cast weak sunlight into their front room, and just into the edge of their kitchen.

She sipped her coffee and said good morning to Tim.

"Feels like that morning at Martha's Vineyard, doesn't it? I sure would love to go back there sometime."

Tim didn't say anything. He just flashed her a quick, strained smile over his shoulder before turning back to the stove top. Meg wanted to ask what was wrong, but she reached for the paper first. Her hand stopped when his shaking voice broke the silence.

"Some heavy news, Meg. It looks really bad," Tim said. He had his back to her, so she couldn't see his face, but the sound of his voice told her enough. Her husband wasn't one to play games with serious news.

Meg flipped the paper over and nearly spilled her coffee.

"An outbreak of Ebola? In Chicago?"

"Worse than that. Much worse," Tim said. He dished up the omelet onto two plates and came to sit beside her at the counter. Meg noticed the stains under his arms. It was hardly warm enough for him to break a sweat, even in front of the stove. She put her arm around his shoulders. They read the article together, and with each paragraph Meg found herself less and less hungry until she simply couldn't think about food at all.

"People attacking each other? Eating—This sounds like something out of a horror movie."

"It is, Meg," Tim said. His voice still shook, and Meg could see tears beginning to leak from his eyes. His lips quivered and he said, "Maybe we should leave. We could stay with my parents in Katonah. I—"

"Leave? Tim, I'm a firefighter. My whole job is to keep people safe. Why would you suggest that?"

Tim looked at her; his eyes hung heavy with worry and

something she'd not seen in them since September of 2001.

"What are you afraid of, Tim? The article didn't say it was spreading. It's in Chicago. The news is terrible, sure, but it's not here. Not yet anyway. And if it does get this far, I can't be in Katonah. I have to help."

"I know, Meg. I know. But I worry this is more than Ebola. You haven't seen the news on TV yet."

He got up and went to the living room, half stumbling. Meg stood to follow him and felt a pull from the windows. She looked outside. What she saw made her freeze, and then she was running for Tim, tackling him to the floor. They landed in a heap on the carpet. Meg slid off him and tugged him behind the sofa.

With a frantic breath, Tim whispered to her. "Are they outside? It's here, isn't it?"

Meg couldn't speak. She didn't have words for what she'd seen out their window. And she hoped it had been her imagination. Some kind of weird hallucination from having read the article.

Monsters aren't real, Meg Pratt. They're not real. They're not.

Her grandfather's voice came to her, with memories from her childhood visits to her grandparents' home. She'd wake up from nightmares and huddle under the blankets, whimpering until Grandma and Grandpa came to soothe her fears.

"Meg?" Tim asked, nearly whimpering himself now.

She risked a look over the sofa and out the window. It was still there. A writhing, contorted monster of a woman. Her tracksuit was in tatters and her mottled flesh was wrapped around her muscles. The woman's skin was different shades of brown and white it seemed, and then

Meg realized what she was seeing.

The woman had been cut or stabbed, almost all over her body. Blood had dried around her wounds, giving them the appearance of bruises. But the rest of her skin… It was like porcelain, but stained and lined with bulging veins that stood out starkly against the pale flesh.

"I have to help her," Meg said. "She needs—"

"No!" Tim shouted, grabbing hold of Meg's arms. He pulled her back down beside him and looked her in the eye. His lips parted as if he'd say something, but only a hushed *Don't* came out.

"Tim, I have to. Someone has to."

"Meg, it's here. You didn't see what I saw on TV. This isn't Ebola. It's a plague from hell."

Meg lifted her head up to check on the woman outside. She peered around the couch, but the woman was gone. Meg shook out of Tim's hands and went in a crouch to the windows. She couldn't see the woman anywhere. Tim whispered behind her, calling her back. She waved a hand for him to be quiet and stay where he was.

The street outside was empty. Then she heard the squeal of car tires and the roar of a revving engine from up the road. A pickup truck came into view, tearing down the street and vanishing around the next corner. Another truck followed it, moving slower, and this one had a man in the bed holding an assault rifle.

What the hell?

As the vehicle passed Meg's house, the man shifted his position in the truck bed so he could aim across the street. He fired at something Meg couldn't see. Then she could see it, and felt her heart trying to leap out of her chest.

The woman was back with three men, all covered with patches of bloodied white flesh. Except now Meg could see their faces. Their mouths were all open in an ugly O-shape, and their eyes…

How is that possible?

The man in the truck shot at them, hitting the woman in the chest and face. She went down in a tangle of bloodied limbs, thrashing ands screaming as she fell. The man next to her went down, too, screeching and clawing at his wounds.

Meg looked for the others, but they had moved so fast she couldn't see where they went. Then one of them was on the truck's cab and leaping onto the man with the assault rifle. It landed on him and tore at his back with its bare hands. Blood spattered out and the man arched away from his attacker.

Meg heard his scream and watched in horror as the fourth infected person launched into the air from where he'd climbed onto a parked car. He flew with a grace and precision Meg had only seen in monster movies, where everything was CGI.

But this was real. Meg knew it. This was really happening right outside their front windows. Big, glass windows with nothing between them and the lawn that stretched from her and Tim's home to the sidewalk like a welcome mat.

Meg spun around in a panic. She knew how to handle emergencies, but this was more than she'd ever dealt with. "We have to get upstairs, Tim. The attic is the only safe place in the house."

She had his wrist and pulled him to his feet. They raced toward the hall leading to their bedroom. They reached the hall at the same time as Meg heard a pounding and scrabbling on the front door. Wood splintered and a man yelled for help.

His voice came into the house, but he wasn't inside yet.

Meg stopped with one hand on the wall. Tim hissed at her to keep going, but her instinct was to go to whoever was outside calling for help.

"Tim, go get the trauma kit from the bathroom. Please—"

The sound of breaking wood interrupted her, followed by another scream for help. Meg caught Tim by the shoulders.

"Go to the bedroom. Hide in the closet. I'm going to help him."

"No, Meg! No. You can't!"

The man who had come inside was groaning in the entryway to their home. Meg heard what sounded like slaps and kicks against wood, like the man was thrashing around on the floor. Then he screamed.

"Help me! Help—I can't stop them!"

Meg and Tim stayed still, out of view of the front door. With a gentle tug, Meg coaxed Tim further down the hall, keeping her hands on his shoulders so they faced each other as they moved. She stepped backwards and felt with her foot along the wall until she came to the guest bathroom.

Tim's face was wet and twisted with fear. His eyes darted left and right. Meg kept one hand on his shoulder and put the other on the handle to the bathroom door.

She gave him her eyes to focus on and tried to smile, so he could have something to trust.

That's what he needs right now. He needs to trust you. That you can save him. Because you can, Meg. Nothing's going to slow you down.

The man came around the corner behind Tim, and Meg felt her stomach heave with fright. Whatever hope she had of saving them vanished.

Blood streamed from the man's eyes, which had turned from white to a sickly yellow.

"Help—Help me, please. You have to help me."

He grunted and doubled over. Tim spun around and backed up against Meg. He put his arms out to protect her, forcing her to stay behind him.

"You have to leave," he said. "You are not well. You have to leave."

Tim's dominant tone startled Meg. She'd never heard him act so aggressively before. When he stepped away from her, still with his arms out, Meg relaxed and let him go. She'd always been the one to act, but he was taking the lead now.

"Hey," Tim said again. He was closer to the man, who was still crouched in the hall, holding his hands against his stomach. He lifted up as Tim came within arm's reach and Meg screamed.

The man's mouth had changed; it bristled with spiny teeth.

He looks like some kind of lamprey. Like he'll—

"Tim!" Meg screamed as the sick man vomited blood straight into her husband's face.

Tim fell backwards, clutching his face and swiping at the blood. He spit up himself then. It had to just be reflex, but still Meg instantly backed away. She knew he had to be infected.

It's blood borne. Whatever this is, it's in the blood.

Tim rolled onto his back and began to spasm. His eyes flicked open and shut and then he was screaming. Both men raked at their own flesh, and swatted at the air like it was full of wasps.

Hallucinations. Oh shit. Oh shit.

The guest bathroom was the closest door and Meg piled into it, slamming it shut and locking it in the same motion. She sat against the vanity sink and held her feet against the door in the darkness.

Outside, she heard more screaming and sounds like arms and legs were slamming into the walls and floor. Then a fierce, high-pitched shriek cut the air.

— 2 —

Jed was running, getting his legs loose and warm, as the sun came up over the rooftops. He'd just done a solid twenty-four hour duty at the stash house, keeping watch over the cotton and other gear. Jed's homie, and newest employer, Chips, was running along with him. Chips kept pace like he'd been running all his life, and Jed even had to put on a little extra steam to keep up with his friend.

"Yo, homie, slow it down a bit. Ain't even had my coffee yet. I'll fall out you keep up that pace."

"Hah!" Chips laughed at him. "You got this, *amigo*. I bet you run like this every morning in the army, huh?"

"I was in the Marines, man," Jed said.

"Whatever, man; you been away for, like, three years. I'm supposed to remember what you signed up for? Shit."

"Five years," Jed said, not missing a beat.

"Okay. Five. What'd you do anyway? You never said. They send you over to the desert? Kill some Al Qaeda?"

Chips didn't need to know what Jed had been doing

9

since he left the suck. At first, it was easy to dodge the questions. But Chips had bugged Jed all night at the stash house, riding him with questions and jabs about what he did after he enlisted.

"I went over there. Fuckin' sandbox. Now I'm just doing my thing, man. You know. Five years in. Now I'm back."

"Huh. Bet you still got sand up in your ass, too."

Jed chuckled and turned so Chips wouldn't see his mouth shaking. He couldn't show or tell Chips what he'd really been doing since he joined the Corps. Or since he got kicked out of it.

But Chips still wasn't satisfied, and kept at him.

"So you back for real? Like you out for good?"

Jed sucked in a few deep breaths and upped their pace a bit himself. He let the question hang in the air between them as they ran. It was the question Chips kept hitting him with, ever since he'd come home.

Home. Like I got one here or anywhere else on this damn planet.

"Yeah, I'm done with the Corps, man. You eat the apple, but fu—"

A car swerved out of an alley up ahead and came roaring down the street past them. Jed and Chips had to jump to the side to avoid getting run down.

"Crazy motherfucker!" Jed hollered after the car as it sped away.

Chips shook his head and tapped Jed on the shoulder. "Let's go, man. We still got about a mile to home."

Jed did a quick sprint to get back into rhythm before he settled down to a steady pace. Chips was right alongside him, and for a second Jed thought his homie would hit him with questions again, but Chips stayed quiet. Jed was grateful, both for being let off the hook about his past and for the chance to just think about what the hell he was doing with his life now.

The Corps didn't want him, so they sent him back to Georgia. And all Georgia had was crystal and cotton to offer. Jed got in with a guy who sold to the high school kids. He made a few bills every week. Then he got rolled for his wad.

Then Jed did a short trip inside on a possession charge. Jed got lucky they didn't slam him for intent to sell to minors.

The fuck didn't Jed do? Jed didn't get his shit together, that's what.

Fucking parole officer hounding him every week, sometimes every day. Making Jed score for him so he could resell the gear to pay for his girlfriend's apartment. Did he let Jed touch it ever? Even a little?

Nope.

And then the parole officer started coming around every *day*. Jed's mom decided she didn't want him either. So she sent him up to his grandma's in New York.

Go on back to New York. Go back to where you really come from.

He'd lived with his grandma in high school, and she still had his room set up the way he'd left it. He was out of the suck, out of Georgia. And out of options.

On cue, Chips fired up the question engine again, like he was reading Jed's damn mind.

"So that's it, man, huh? You just out?"

"Yeah," he said to Chips as they ran. "I'm out, man. Out for good."

"What happened? They find out you just a punk from the block?"

Jed swallowed hard and kept his hands loose. The urge to ball his fists and rock Chips's world flamed fierce in his chest, but he fought it down and stayed cool. He needed his homie now more than ever. If it meant taking a few shots Chips didn't know he was giving, so be it.

They ran a little ways more and the city's silence hung over them like a cloud. In the weird quiet, Jed found his voice.

"I got hit."

"Shut the fuck up," Chips said. His voice was all calm and casual, like he figured Jed was joking. "Where? How'd it go down?"

Jed was ready for that one. He'd practiced this part of the story. Every night in his head before he went to sleep in his cell. On the plane, too. The one that carried him home with his bad conduct discharge papers in his pocket.

"We were doing this patrol, you know? Fucking Al-Qaeda don't play games. We lost half our guys. Got all split up and crazy. Then it's just me and this kid from some flyover state. Farm boy. He's pissing in his clothes, right? Like he's gonna start crying for momma. And I can see the LT. The lieutenant, you—"

"I know what a LT is, homie," Chips said. Jed looked at him, thinking maybe he'd played it wrong, but Chips was staring straight ahead, pumping his arms and running, with his face all slack, like he was someplace else inside his mind.

"Yeah. So the LT is on the ground out there. He's holding his stomach. I see his guts hanging out. But he's moving. Farm boy, he's fucking useless. So it's on me. I crawl out and the bullets keep coming. But they miss me, man."

"They missing you," Chips said, like it was a church sermon Jed was giving and Chips was repeating all the holy parts.

"Yeah. They miss me. Then I get to the LT, and he's shot bad. Stomach all torn up. But I pull him out of there. Bullets still coming in. Still missing me. Then I have to get up on my knees. I drag the LT around the corner. Right when I do that, I feel it."

The city was still silent, and Jed felt something tug inside his mind. There should be a lot more cars on the road, trucks and busses. People everywhere. It wasn't that late in the morning, but it was late enough.

But New York City wasn't screaming and roaring like the monster Jed knew it was.

"Yo, Chips. You think maybe something's going down? Shit's all quiet, man."

Chips just stared at the road ahead, off in some world Jed could only imagine.

The hell's going on? Why's it so quiet?

"You feel it," Chips said, shaking Jed out of his thoughts. "What it's like, homie? Getting shot? What it's like?"

"You ain't been shot yet?" Jed asked, surprised. The way Chips and his brothers used to run before Jed enlisted, he figured the guy would have taken some lead by now.

Chips still wasn't saying anything, just running and staring at the city in front of him. Jed thought he should ask again, but decided to keep on with his story. The city was still weirdly quiet, but it had given Jed just the thing he was looking for: a place to stop running and maybe even pick up something to take the edge off of his day.

"Yo, let's hold up here, at the corner store. I'll show you."

They brought their run down to a trot and paced around the sidewalk in front of the store.

"We should pick up a couple bottles. Some fortified sound good to you?" Jed asked.

Chips shook his head and leaned down, resting his hands on his knees. "Nah, homie. I'm off that shit. Only drink mezcal now. But I thought you gonna show me where you got shot. Let's see it, Jarhead Jed."

Jed sniffed and resisted the urge to clock his friend right there. If he was going to make it with Chips and his crew, Jed had to get his cred. So he pulled his shirt up until he revealed a quarter-sized scar over his ribs on his left side.

"Right there, yo," he said.

Chips leaned in to look at it and his eyes bugged out a little. Then Chips laughed and slapped Jed on the shoulder.

"*Amigo!* You hard, man. You hard!"

Jed dropped his shirt and said he had to take a piss.

"Bet they let you use it inside," Chips said, aiming a thumb at the corner store. "Dude who runs this place used to be in the army. Went to Panama. He hook you up, I bet."

They went to the tinted glass door and pushed it open, but it stopped against something. Jed gave it a shove and the door slid farther in, and Jed felt something heavy sliding behind it. The place was a wreck, like straight out of some zombie movie. Blood stains covered everything, and the shelves were ate up like hell.

"The fuck happened here?" Chips asked.

The cash register was on its side behind the bullet-proof glass at the counter. Coins spilled all over the place back there. A blood stained dollar bill flapped in the breeze of a little electric fan that sat next to a stack of porno mags behind the glass.

Jed looked down at the floor, behind the door they'd shoved open. That's when he saw the first zombie. Except it wasn't like the kind in the movies. He wasn't sure it was even a zombie at all. It looked more like a monster.

The skin was all white and gross, and the veins bulged out around the muscles. The face was ripped up and bloody, like it had been blasted by a shotgun. But the mouth was visible. It was different, like a circle of raw puffy pale flesh. And instead of teeth, it had little needles, like spines.

Chips came around Jed's left shoulder and looked down at the thing. "The fuck is that? Shit, homie, we gotta go. We—"

Before Chips could finish, a groan echoed out from the back of the store. Jed went still, and felt ice run through his veins.

"Let's go," he said, tugging on Chips's shoulder. His friend didn't waste a breath. Chips whipped around behind Jed and was out the door running. Another groan came from the back of the store and then a shriek ripped through the air. Jed felt warm piss run down his leg as he sped out of the store, running for his life.

— 3 —

South Jamaica, Queens

Meg heard a horrific clicking and popping sound in the hallway outside the bathroom door. Then more shrieking in short, sharp bursts. Then silence.

Meg closed her eyes.

You don't run from a fire. You run into the fire.

She should go out and help Tim, and the infected man. But she didn't know what they would do to her.

Oh God, Tim's infected!

Would Tim kill the other man? Or would they both come after her? The newspaper said—

Meg felt her legs go weak at the thought. But she had to keep the door closed tight. If it had only been Tim who was infected, maybe she could have helped him. She could restrain him, get him to the hospital. But with two infected people outside the door—and if what the newspapers had said was true…

Get Tim. Get him restrained. Get him to the hospital.

"You're okay, Meg. We'll be okay. We'll be okay."

But how? How do I get out of here and how do I get to Tim?

Meg kept whispering to herself, listening for

movement in the hall. She heard a scratching sound, then a scraping, like when Biggins sharpened his claws on the wood floor. But this was louder. Much louder, and longer.

Another shriek cut the air, followed by the sound of splintering wood again. Howls and screams cascaded through the house, but quickly grew quiet.

They're gone. They left the house.

But she couldn't be sure. If they were still inside and she went out there, she could be infected. Or killed. She had to isolate herself from the pathogen if she was going to be any help.

Tim's face came to her then, like the image of a terrified child. She'd pulled a little boy from a burning house once and he'd looked the same way when she told him it would be all right. He'd been frozen with fear, curled up under his bed. But he came out, shaking and sobbing.

She'd had to chop through a wall to get to him—

"I'm going to get us out of here, Tim. Wherever you are, I'm coming."

Meg waited, listening for sounds of movement in the house. A floorboard creaked. Something scraped, like knives on glass. Another shriek came then, and Meg tensed, waiting for the scraping and clawing sounds to get closer.

But they didn't. If Meg's ears could be trusted, whoever or whatever had come inside, they were leaving the house again. A shriek came, and she heard a rapid scrabbling, like the cat racing for the dinner bowl at mealtime. The scraping and clawing sounds faded away after a bit, leaving Meg tense in the dark and tiny sanctuary of the bathroom.

Quiet seconds passed with Meg calming her breathing until she heard more screams and howls from outside.

After a few more breaths, Meg released her legs from holding the door closed. She settled back against the vanity. In a quick motion, Meg turned, climbed onto the vanity, and put a foot on either side of the sink. She reached for the ceiling fan cover and worked it loose. It came free, but slipped from her fingers and clattered on the floor.

Waiting to ensure no other sounds came from inside the house, Meg gripped the drywall next to the ceiling fan and yanked hard. A piece of it came away, showering dust and tufts of pink insulation onto her head. Meg turned her face down just in time to avoid a mouthful of the debris.

Ignoring the fear in her gut that told her she would be heard, Meg kept at it. She yanked another chunk off the ceiling and then another, dropping the pieces now as fast as she could, and doing her best to let the insulation fall on the outside of her shirt. She felt the sting of the fiberglass against her skin, but most of it landed in her hair or tumbled off her shoulders.

Finally she had a hole big enough to climb through. But she still had to push aside the plywood boards they used to create a floor in the attic. Meg hoped she hadn't dug her escape route under the heaviest boxes up there, or this would be the shortest exit strategy ever.

Working one hand into the narrow gap between the pieces of plywood, Meg wrapped her fingers over the rafter beside the ceiling fan. Making sure she had a good hold, Meg hoisted herself with the hand on the rafter and pushed against the board with her free hand. It moved only a little and dropped back down just as fast.

Shit.

She had found the heaviest boxes after all. But the board moved, so she could get out if she worked at it.

"Nothing's going to slow you down," Meg's grandmother said in her mind. The mantra kept her going during Ironman races, and she forced herself to chant it under her breath now.

"Nothing's going to slow you down, Meg. Nothing."

She hoisted herself once more and pushed again. The board moved and slammed back down. She did it again, pushing up and then flexing her wrist to the side when she was at the peak of her reach.

The board slammed down, but it had shifted. Meg kept it up. Hoist, push, flex. Hoist, push, flex. Each time the board came back down, Meg worried she wouldn't be able to get it to move again. But it did move, until she finally had a good six-inch gap between it and the next board.

With a grunt, Meg used all her strength to shove the board aside. It moved slowly, inch by painful inch. Her shoulder was on fire from the strain of holding herself up with just the tips of her toes on the vanity. The board slid to the side, and then she felt the weight shift suddenly, followed by a heavy thud on the ceiling beside her.

A scrabbling sound came to her ears from somewhere in the house. Had they heard her? Were they coming back?

Meg listened. The scraping sounds came through the walls, and a kind of popping or clicking, like a ratchet slowly rotating. The gap above her head wasn't big enough to get through yet. She lifted up, on her toes, and gave another shove against the board. It moved aside and she could see a thin line of light against the inside of the attic roof.

Meg climbed up into the close, dark space with only slivers of light creeping in from the one small window at the end of the attic. They had so many boxes up here it was a wonder any light got in at all. Meg slid her escape hatch closed behind her and replaced the heavy boxes on top of it.

When she looked around her hiding place, Meg's heart sank.

What have I done? I haven't helped anyone but myself.

"Oh, Tim," Meg said, worried now that her husband might be losing his sanity. If the virus acted as fast as she'd seen, what would be left of him even if they did get to a hospital? His brain could boil away from fever before—

"Someone will come," she said, forcing calm into her chest. "Help is on the way. It has to be."

Meg's breathing slowed, but she still felt guilty that she wasn't out there bringing that help where it was needed right now. There had to be people who needed medical attention. Emergency crews would—

Why haven't they called me yet?

Her fear magnified until it felt like she would suffocate under it, trapped in the attic and with no one to call or any way to get out. Meg practiced her breathing exercises, relaxing her chest and abdomen, letting the tension out of her shoulders and arms.

A scraping along the roof shook Meg from her calm. Then a ghastly shriek sounded out and was answered by more calls from nearby. Including one inside the house, under her feet. She felt it move, whatever it was, scampering away from her and going into the bedroom below. Then she heard the shattering of glass and more screams from outside the house.

Meg flinched with every sound that reached her ears. Even the tiniest creak set her off, fighting down the urge to panic. She shook her head to clear her vision as the room went dim around her. Meg blinked and turned, slowly, to look down the length of the attic space.

Even with the boxes in the way, Meg couldn't help but see the dark shape moving outside the window.

But that means they're on the wall outside. They can climb walls!

Tim's voice came through the boards beneath her.

"Mee-eg. Help mee-e. Hel—"

He coughed and Meg heard retching sounds below. Another voice was added to his. Then someone screamed in agony and Meg heard gunshots as the snarling and shrieking sounds moved through the house and toward the front door.

"Tim!" she yelled, dashing on her hands and knees, following the sound beneath her toward the end of the attic. But it was too late. Meg could see him outside now, through the attic window. Tim raced across their front lawn with another infected person.

They moved in a crouch, on all fours, and their arms and legs seemed to have extra joints in them, almost whirling in their motion as Tim and the other one galloped across the lawn. They darted side to side in a zig zag as they chased a police officer who had her gun out. The woman screamed and fired behind her as she ran.

Meg cried out when Tim tackled the officer and latched his mouth onto her neck. Blood sprayed out onto the street and the other infected person raced up to join Tim as they—

Oh, God. They're…they're feeding.

— 4 —

Jed caught up to Chips at the next block. Together, they raced away from the screams and shrieks that split the quiet air around the neighborhood. They juked through alleyways and down streets choked with cars stopped in the middle of the road. He spotted a couple nice rides all the way up on the sidewalk, like they'd been crashed there.

"Chips, we should grab one of these rides man."

"I ain't stopping for shit. Just keep running."

Jed kept pace with his friend. Two blocks along, he was about to argue about getting a car again when Chips split off the street and dashed into the side yard of a boarded up house.

"Yo, where you going?" Jed yelled, chasing after him.

Chips didn't say anything, just sped off around the back of the house. Jed followed and rounded the corner just as Chips was lifting a board away from a basement window.

"C'mon," Chips said. "This another stash house. We can hide out."

Jed came up beside Chips and helped move the thick plywood out of the way. A rope that was dangling from one corner of the board kept getting tangled around Jed's arms. He had to swat it aside twice before he could get a grip on the board. He nearly lost it when an animal shriek sounded from a few yards over.

The sound of breaking glass and a few gunshots followed. Then a scream and some wet noises. Jed didn't want to think about what the noises meant. He just wanted to get inside, but the damn rope kept twisting in his sweaty hands and he couldn't get it off of him.

"Help me, man!"

Chips reached over and slapped Jed's hands aside. He grabbed the rope and coiled it in a couple of quick motions.

"Get inside, homie," Chips said, jerking his chin toward the basement window.

Jed dropped to his stomach and crawled backwards through the small window. He dropped into the damp basement and fell back on his ass. Chips's feet stuck through the window. Then he was down and still holding the rope. Jed looked back at the window.

"How we gonna close it up?"

Chips tugged on the rope, hand over hand, until the board moved back in place, covering the window and blocking all the light out of the basement.

"Flashlight is on the box behind you, homie," Chips said. "Get it lit so I can put the rope back."

Jed felt around in the dark until he bumped against a wooden crate. He was sweating like mad from the run, and the adrenaline rush of being chased by monsters. His hands shook, and his breathing came in ragged, short gasps.

"Yo, Jed," Chips said right behind him. Jed jerked to the side and yelped.

"Fuck! You scared the shit out of me, man. Don't do that. Please."

"Yeah, yeah. Okay, man. Okay. I get the light."

Jed heard Chips patting the wooden crate, and then a light flared in the darkness, showing the inside of the basement. Chips had an electric Coleman lantern in one hand and a gun in the other.

"The hell you get that from?" Jed asked.

"This our home away from home. Got everything we need here."

Chips tucked the gun into his pants and went back to the rope.

"Yo, come hold the light for me," he said.

Jed went up and took the lantern from his friend. He watched as Chips wrapped the rope around a peg stuck in the wall and then fastened it there with a clasp attached to a spring.

"You pull the rope on the outside and the little thing lets go," he said.

"Pretty tight, man."

"C'mon upstairs. Gotta get you a piece."

Chips led the way up a set of narrow wooden steps to a door that opened into what used to be a kitchen. A busted porcelain sink hung off its pipes against a wall, underneath some windows. But the place didn't have any counters or cabinets, and the floor was tore up like hell.

"Man," Jed said, "Gunny Bayles would tear hell through whoever shammed off this detail."

"¿*Que?* The fuck you talking about?" Chips asked.

"My old platoon sergeant. Gunny Bayles. He was always on us—"

"Man, I don't need to hear about some *pinche gringo culero* who ain't here now and wouldn't help us even if he was. I thought you was out anyway, homie. The fuck you talkin' about that dude for? He gonna come save your ass? That what you think?"

Chips had gone through the kitchen to the next room. Jed went in, ready to give Chips some shit for lighting into him like that. Chips was on his knees. He'd pulled up a floorboard and was digging around in the space below. The room, like the kitchen, was bare bones. Nothing in it but dust and dirt, and his friend. Except Chips wasn't looking like much of a friend now. His hair was slick with sweat from their run, and every time Jed met his eyes, Chips held his face in a wince, like he couldn't wait to get clear of Jed.

"Dude, chill. I was just remembering, okay?"

"Yeah, you was remembering. Well remember who got your back, Jed. Remember that, huh? Here, take this."

Chips held out a black pistol with a square slide, all boxy like the one Jed's parole officer used to carry.

Jed accepted the gun from Chips and hefted it in his hands. It felt thick in his grip, even more than the M9 he'd held once.

"That's a Glock, homie," Chips said. "You gotta watch—"

The gunshot clapped in Jed's ears and he nearly lost his grip on the gat. For a second he was back in Iraq, remembering the one time he'd heard gunfire close up that wasn't on a shooting range. His ears rang with a steady hum that grew and then slowly went quiet.

"Yo, Jed," Chips said. His eyes were wider now. "You cool, man?"

Jed felt cool. The bullet hole in the floor told him different, but at least he hadn't shot Chips. "Yeah, m'cool. I'm just a little wired up is all. Ain't held a piece since the sandbox. And this shit outside man. I don't know—"

Chips put a hand out to take the gun and Jed passed it over. He watched while Chips cleared the weapon. He passed it back to Jed.

"Like I was sayin', you gotta watch the trigger. That *chingadera* right there. That's your safety, homie."

Jed looked carefully at the weapon and saw the little half-trigger poking out from the real one.

"Okay, man. Can I have the ammo back?"

Chips tossed him the magazine and Jed slotted it home. He was about to rack the slide to charge the weapon, but Chips gave him a look.

"Yeah. Better safe than sorry, huh?"

"You speak true, *cabrón*," Chips said. He stood up and went to a hallway that led out of the room. "We can go out the front door. It got a lock on it."

"Cool, but hey, man, I gotta take a dump. The toilets work in this heap?"

"Over there," Chips said, pointing to a door that hung half off its hinges. "Make it quick, *amigo*. We gotta get back to my place. Make sure my little brothers are okay."

Jed went to the bathroom and heard Chips walking into a room at the front of the house, saying he'd be waiting for him by the door.

In the bathroom, Jed put the Glock on the counter by

the sink, next to a roll of toilet paper with just enough on it for his needs. He dropped his pants and flopped down on the seat, wrapping his arms around himself. He felt the scar under his left arm.

Jed remembered the burning sensation against his ribs. And he remembered the cigar that his squad leader held pressed against a hundred dollar bill that he'd laid up tight against Jed's skin.

That was Jed's first night in Iraq. He'd been assigned to a platoon that had lost almost half their men the week before. They were at that fucking Camp Baharia place…

They called it *Dreamland* when he got there. Everybody said he'd spend every day wishing he could just wake the fuck up back at home. Jed blew it off, saying he'd been waiting for a chance to show Al-Qaeda how he felt about what they did to New York.

But the other guys were right. Jed didn't get twenty minutes at *Dreamland* before he wanted to leave.

The platoon was picking up newbies. Jed and ten others guys. They all got in a line and the squad leaders picked them one by one. Jed and one other guy were in 3rd Squad. The other guy was a bible thumper, and he looked like an all-American kid from next door. All square chin, blond hair and shit, praying every night and probably helping old ladies cross the street before he signed up.

The blond kid with the chin got in easy. Everybody liked him right off. But the squad leader had a test for Jed, to prove he could be a Marine like the rest of them.

Just a way to give a man his cred. Fucking assholes.

Jed figured he was wearing the uniform, so that was proof enough. Hell, he'd signed up for the suck just like they all had. But the other guys wanted to test him.

"Okay, Welch," the sergeant said. *"You keep it there until the cigar burns through, you can have the c-note."*

Funny motherfucker. Jed went along with the bet, thinking it wouldn't take that long. Most that might happen is he'd get a little red mark and then he'd be a hundred bucks richer and be done with the *proving himself* bullshit.

But money don't burn like that, do it? It don't burn if you don't let any oxygen get behind the bill. Just hold it tight to your brother's skin and watch him squirm until he can't take it anymore. Then you laugh like a bitch while he goes looking for the burn ointment.

"Funny motherfucker," Jed said to himself, remembering how everyone had laughed at him. After that, Jed figured a bad conduct discharge was his only ticket home. Either that or a long black bag with a zipper down the front.

Chips is right. Those assholes wouldn't have my back if shit went down.

Chips' voice broke in on Jed's memories.

"Yo, Jed. Pinch it off, *cabrón.*"

Jed finished his business and flushed.

When he heard Chips screaming for him to hurry, Jed nearly fell over his own feet trying to get his pants on and grab the Glock at the same time.

"Jed! Get the fuck up here. We got trouble—"

Then he heard gunfire from the front of the house and felt his heart jump into his throat.

— 5 —

Meg refused to watch what was happening below her hiding place. She wasn't worried about being seen, though. If the monsters could still think at all, they would find her. Her end would come just as quickly as Tim's had. She sat back, landing on her hip and sliding away from the window, no longer thinking about getting Tim to a hospital or about anything other than how unfair it all was.

I could have helped. It didn't have to be like this.

She had lost her husband. He was dead, gone forever and replaced by a horrific monster. But as far away as she moved from the window, she couldn't escape the growling and sucking sounds that mixed with cries and moans coming from the street outside.

Tears flooded Meg's vision and she clapped her hands over her ears to hide from the horror show that her world had become. In her mind's eye, she saw monsters roaming the streets, and leaping like demons from cars onto walls and rooftops. The beasts smashed their way into homes and dragged the innocent into the streets to

33

be broken and devoured, and Meg could do nothing to stop it.

Her heart beat a staccato against her ribs, and the pummeling sounds from below kept ringing in her ears. The blows came to her in a steady punching rhythm. *Chop-chop-chop-chop. Pop-pop-pop. Chop*—

Meg wiped at her eyes. That was gunfire. It had to be. A second later, and Meg was moving cautiously back to the window. The sounds had stopped. Now she heard shrieks, but also shouting.

A lot of shouting. Men giving orders in between bursts of gunfire. Meg risked a look outside but stayed back from the window in case the one on the wall was still out there. Smears and sprays of blood decorated the street. The dead police officer lay on their lawn, but she saw no sign of Tim or the other monsters. Shaking, and half afraid that one of them would crash in to attack her, Meg leaned close against the window. She tried to get a view in every direction she could.

The street seemed empty. She couldn't hear any of the tell tale scraping or clicking sounds that signaled the monsters' movement. And the only shrieks she heard came from further down the street. In a split second, Meg was back at the heavy boxes and pushing them out of the way. She shoved them aside, not caring that they slammed and banged against the boards.

Meg breathed in deep and put her feet at the edge of the plywood covering the hole she'd come in through. With a quick shove, the board moved and Meg whipped her legs up and away, rolling to her side in case one of them was down there.

She came up against more boxes and scrambled to get

a good position to defend herself with a kick in case anything popped up from the bathroom below. The room was still dark below her. The bathroom door was still closed.

Something moved inside the house, though. Something big, scraping along the wooden floors.

What if it's Tim? What if he's come back for you?

Nothing moved in the hall. No shrieks of recognition, nothing to signal that prey had been found. Then the house seemed to go quiet altogether.

It's gone. It's gone and you're good. Now go!

Meg shook herself. She couldn't allow for the luxury of worry or fear. People needed help out there, and that meant she had to act. Meg moved to the hole and dropped slowly, setting her feet on the vanity first.

All the noise she heard was from outside the house. Meg opened the bathroom door and stepped into the hall. The house was quiet. And it felt empty. She moved to their bedroom at the back, to the sliding glass door. Glass littered the carpet everywhere, in splinters and shards as big as her arm. Biggins was nowhere to be seen, but there wasn't any blood either. She hoped he'd gotten away.

Meg grabbed a towel from the linen chest beside their bed and used it to pick up the most sword-like piece of glass she could find. It might not save her if she were attacked, but it felt good to have some kind of weapon in her hand.

The backyard was quiet as far as she could tell. Nothing seemed to be moving out there. Meg stepped to the broken door and kicked out the remaining bits of glass that might cut her if she had to get back in quickly.

When she'd made a clear path for herself, she looked left and right quickly before whipping back inside. She hadn't seen anything, but better safe than sorry.

You're good. Everything is okay.

Meg chanted her grandmother's comforting words in her mind as she went back to the doorway and stepped outside. For the first time she caught the reek of rotten fruit and realized she'd been smelling it as she made her way through the house. It had been faint inside, but out here it came to her like a wave of funk from a dumpster on a hot city day.

Gunshots peppered the neighborhood around her, along with the occasional shriek or squeal of the monsters. Meg didn't hear any more human screams, though.

If she could find the police, maybe they could get her somewhere safe.

And somewhere she could start to help.

Meg winced when she heard a scream of terror from across the back yard. Their neighbors had never been nice people, but they didn't deserve this. Nobody did. The screams continued and then stopped abruptly. Were they dead? Were they like Tim? What if they were just hurt? If Meg could get to them, maybe she could help.

Or maybe you could get eaten alive.

She let the piece of glass fall from her hand and shatter on the patio beside her feet. Tim was dead, he had to be. And so were the neighbors. Ripped apart by monsters that shouldn't exist. What the hell was she supposed to do now? Who could she help when even that cop and the guy with an assault rifle weren't able to defend themselves from these things?

Meg heard gunshots nearby, and more shrieks from the monsters. They sounded inhuman, like animals, but not any kind of animal Meg had ever heard before. She glanced at the neighbors' place. Through their patio door she could see bodies on their bedroom floor. Splattered blood dripped from the glass door. As Meg watched, a spray of blood covered the glass, and then another. Meg reeled away and ducked down behind the shrubs that divided the yards. More gunshots came from the street outside, and shouting that sounded like someone from the army was out there.

"Corporal Parvil! Take Sims, and Olafoe. Clear that side. High and low, watch the rooftops. Cantrell, Jackson, on me. Clear this street and rally at the trucks."

Meg heard a chorus of grunts that sounded like agreements. Should she go out and ask for help? What if they thought she was one of the monsters and shot her?

Her grandmother's mantra came back to her again. *"You're good."*

With a shaking hand, Meg reached for the broken glass again. But it was all little pieces now. Useless as a weapon unless she was going to use it on herself.

No! You're good, Meg. You're good.

She stayed hidden. Then she poked her head out from around the bushes and pulled back fast. She hadn't seen any soldiers on the street or in the neighbors yards. Or any monsters. But she could hear them a few yards over. And they were in her neighbors' house just behind her.

They are *monsters now. They're not your neighbors anymore.*

Meg stepped out of her hiding place, keeping her hands in front of her and flicking her gaze to either side as she moved. She lifted her foot for one more step when she heard shattering glass from a patio door nearby. A shriek cut the air and gunfire followed. Meg ducked down and ran, following the wall of their house. She kept her head down, but tried to get a look at where the soldiers might have gone.

She moved down the driveway and spotted the soldiers across the street. Meg kept moving, looking back the way she'd come and then quickly at the street again, until she came to a stop behind their garbage cans. Three soldiers moved on the other side of the street, crouched low and with their weapons aimed up and at eye level. They switched their aim as they moved, up and down, at the rooftops and back to their level on the street. One of them raced up to a door that had been broken in and shouted something into the house. Then he lifted something from his belt and threw it inside.

Seconds later Meg flinched as an explosion sent glass and dust flying out of the windows of the house. The soldiers all rushed inside and Meg heard gunfire. Flashes of light flickered in the windows of the house. She was so transfixed she almost missed hearing the scraping and clicking sounds behind her. Meg spun around. Tim was clawing his way toward her.

But he wasn't the man she used to know. Not anymore.

Tim's once bronzed flesh had gone almost chalky white. His fingers had grown into claws that scratched on the concrete, and his face–

Oh, God, what happened to you, Tim?

— 6 —

Elmhurst, Queens

Up at the front door, Chips was popping caps at something outside. He fired through a little square peephole that was cut into the door. The window next to the door was boarded up, but it had a panel, about the same size as the hole Chips was shooting through. Jed went up next to Chips and opened the panel. One of the zombie things was out there, snarling and spitting. It had blood all down its front, and its clothes were shredded, like it had been locked in a bear cage.

But its face... Jed couldn't get the image out of his mind, the sucker mouth dripping with spit and blood, and those little needle teeth.

Chips kept busting rounds out the peephole in the door but he couldn't get a good bead on the thing outside. It moved so fast, all jerky and quick, and with its joints clicking and popping like a socket wrench. In a flash it jumped forward and slammed against the door, knocking Chips' gun out of his hand. He ducked down to grab it and yelled at Jed.

"Fucking shoot it! Shoot it!"

39

Jed slotted the Glock into the hole in the board and tried to line up the monster in his sights. It was still right up on the door, scratching at the wood with its claws. Jed could see the thing's pale white skin, and its muscles stretched tight like cables around its freaky joints. Every time it moved an arm or a leg, it made that same sickening clicking sound. Jed angled the Glock at it and got off two shots that only pissed it off, just running furrows across its back. Chips was back up and aimed through his peephole. He put one into the monster's head right over its left eye. The head snapped back and the thing went over onto the front walk.

Jed's ears were ringing like mad. He could hardly make out what Chips was saying. His mouth was moving, but all Jed heard was something like *Go shit*. Then Chips had a hand on Jed's shoulder and was spinning him aside. Chips closed the peephole Jed had used and then looked out the one in the door again.

After a few minutes of watching the street, Chips closed his peephole. Jed's ears were settling down a bit, but the steady hum lingered in the background.

"Fucking shit, man," Chips said. "Fucking shit. We gotta get back to my brothers, man. You… Yo, Jed!"

Jed was just staring at the peephole in the door, afraid that any second it would come busting in and one of the monsters would chew his face off.

"Yeah, man. Yeah," he said.

"You wanna get with the fuckin' program, homie? We gotta go."

Chips reached for the doorknob and Jed automatically raised the Glock to cover the entrance. His ears were still ringing bad, but he felt something kick in right then.

They'd trained on clearing buildings back in the Corps. He knew what to do.

"You ready?"

"Yeah, man. Go on three."

Chips counted and wrenched the door open on three. Jed swept the Glock left to right, but the street was empty. The dead thing on the front walk was still dead. Jed forced himself not to look at it and just keep his eyes on the street outside.

"Looks clear man," he said.

"You go first, homie. What's that called? Point?"

"Yeah."

"Cool. You on point."

Chips patted Jed on the shoulder and stepped back so he was in line with him. Jed felt Chips' aim over his right shoulder, so he kept his eyes on their left as they stepped out of the house and around the dead thing on the walk.

"Home is up the street," Chips said. "About four blocks and then left."

Jed nodded and grunted to let Chips know he'd heard him. Then they moved out, first at a slow jog and then picking it up to a sprint when they saw the crawling shapes of monsters on the rooftops down the street, back the way they'd come from the corner store.

At least they're behind us.

A howl went up from the monsters back there, then a shriek followed by what sounded to Jed like a stampede of really big and really angry cats. The clattering of claws and feet on shingles and the tops of cars echoed down the street as Jed and Chips ran like the wind. The things didn't seem to have a line of sight on them, or maybe they did. Jed threw a glance over his shoulder. The monsters crawled over everything, cars, lawns, rooftops. Even if they hadn't spotted Jed and Chips yet, they were definitely coming along their path.

Right before the end of the block, Chips tugged on Jed's shirt and they went into a yard, ducking behind a row of bushes.

"They see us?" Chips asked.

"Fuck, man. I don't know. Why we stopping? We gotta run."

"Shortcut, *cabrón*. This way."

Chips led them around the back of the house. Two boards in the fence had been pulled out to make a path. They raced through it to the other side of the block, coming out between two little houses that were boarded up just like the safe house. But Jed could tell these weren't places they could hide. Old mattresses littered the back yard of one of the houses, along with empty syringes and old condoms. Jed couldn't wait to get away from the place, but Chips put up a hand for him to chill.

"I'ma go check the street. Watch behind us, man."

Chips went up ahead, looking left and right once he got to the front of the house.

"See anything?" Jed asked.

"Nah, man. Looks good."

Jed moved up fast and joined Chips. They stepped out from beside the house and moved to the sidewalk. A little farther down the street, every house had broken windows and streaks of blood around the doors.

"Let's go, man," Jed said, nudging Chips' shoulder.

They moved out at a jog again, picking up speed as they went. The noises of the monsters from one block over kept echoing around the neighborhood. Now and then Jed heard a human scream mixed in with the snarling and howling of the monsters. It was all on the next block, but Jed still didn't dare look behind them. He and Chips just ran full tilt until they got to Chips' apartment building. They ducked behind a hedge and ran along the wall outside the pool area. Chips pulled up at the end of the hedge and scrambled for the top of the wall. Jed went to stuff the Glock into his pants but was afraid he'd blow his own junk off, so he waited until Chips was up top so he could hand the piece up.

He got up the wall and down the other side where Chips was waiting with the Glock held out.

"Not bad, homie. You run like that when 5-0 after us, you gonna do fine with my crew."

Jed almost said he was done with the idea of being in Chips' crew, because he was getting the fuck out of New York now that the zombies were here. But Chips was already walking off around the pool, digging into his pocket for his keys. Jed listened to the neighborhood and scanned the buildings around them. He didn't see any broken windows or smears of blood.

Things seemed cool. As cool as they could be since Jed didn't hear any screams nearby, and the howls and shrieks of the monsters all seemed to be going away from them. But he didn't hear much else either. No cars driving by, no kids yelling in the yards. Then he caught the snaps of small arms fire, and louder explosions like grenades echoing from a few blocks away, maybe farther. Chips had stopped outside the door to his apartment. His eyes locked onto Jed's, like he'd heard it, too.

"That the army?" Chips asked. "See, they gonna take care of the zombies man. It's cool."

"Yeah, maybe so. We should get inside anyway."

Chips opened the door and went inside. Before Jed could get there, the door closed with a *bang*. He went up to the door carefully and listened. He could hear a TV or a radio, but then it cut out. Jed had the Glock out. He scanned the pool area and the nearby buildings. He didn't hear or see anything except the occasional *pop pop pop* of small arms.

Jed had his back to the door. He lifted a hand to knock over his shoulder when the door opened behind him. Jed went to turn around but felt something sharp and cold stick him in the back.

— 7 —

South Jamaica, Queens

Blood leaked from Tim's sickly yellow eyes, and his mouth had formed into a sucker, just like the man in their house. As he moved, Meg heard the joints in his arms and legs crackling like embers popping from a fire. A scream started in Meg's throat, but came out as a choked gasp when one of their neighbors came around the corner of the house. It was the husband. He had blood all over him, but he walked like a normal human.

Tim flinched and spun around, facing the man.

"She was my wife, you fucking animal!" the man roared at Tim.

"Don't—" Meg shouted, but the man had already moved. He jumped at Tim with his face twisted up in a snarl of fury. The man screamed and grabbed at Tim's face with both hands as the two fell together and rolled in a tangle up against the wall. Meg staggered back with one hand wrapped around her middle and the other hand up in front of her mouth. She knew she should help, but couldn't bring herself to move an inch closer.

The neighbor and Tim grappled and it looked like the

man might have the upper hand. His fingers dug into Tim's cheeks, holding the monstrous mouth away from the man's flesh. Then Tim sliced a clawed hand across the man's ribs and Meg gave a startled cry as blood sprayed out and spattered the wall of their house.

It was over a few seconds later. The man lost his grip on Tim's face, and Meg stared in horror as the thing that was her husband latched his sucker mouth onto their neighbor's throat.

Moments later, Tim stopped and flicked his tongue out from between puffy, blood stained lips. Rows of sharp teeth seemed to click together in his mouth, like needles.

He shrieked at her. Then Tim lifted his arm to his mouth and bit down hard, his mouth collapsing around his flesh and sucking. Blood welled and ran down his flesh in dark rivulets.

Meg screamed and ran from the house, falling over her feet and tumbling toward the sidewalk. She heard gunfire again, and what sounded like another small explosion from nearby. Meg caught herself against the curb and rolled onto her side so she could jump up and run. Behind her she heard Tim howling and shrieking, and the gunfire continued. Meg turned around in time to see a police officer in SWAT gear holding an assault rifle. The officer fired and a string of bullet holes appeared across Tim's chest; blood sprouted like blossoms and sprayed out his back to stain the wall of their house even more.

Her will and strength and everything she'd ever believed in fell away in that moment. Watching Tim be taken from her had been horrifying. Seeing what he had become, and watching him die a second time... Meg fell on her side, dropped flat to the ground, and huddled against the curb whimpering and wailing her pain onto the concrete and pavement.

"Ma'am!" a man's voice shouted at her from the street.

Meg cried and screamed as her chest shook under her sobs. She beat a fist against the street and shouted Tim's name.

"Ma'am! Are you okay? Are you infected? Ma'am!"

"No I'm not fucking okay! My husband is dead!" Meg shouted back at whoever was yelling at her. The man was nearby. She could hear his footsteps get closer, but she didn't care what he wanted or who he was. Meg moaned and cried and slapped her hand on the street now, feeling the rough stone surface cut against her palm.

"Ma'am? Are you bitten? Have you come into contact with infected blood?"

Meg opened her eyes and saw a pair of boots through her tears. She lifted her hand slowly and wiped at her eyes. The person in front of her was a soldier, and he had his gun aimed right at her face.

"What the fuck?" Meg screamed, flipping onto her back and putting her hands out in front of her.

"Ma'am, calm down. Are you bitten? Have you been in contact with any of the infected?" He was a dark-skinned young man, with warm brown eyes. Even with the look of fear on his face, Meg felt safe near him.

The tears came back and Meg blubbered through her sobs. "No, I'm not bit—bitten. My husband—"

Meg closed her eyes and cried, letting her hands fall to her sides as she sat against the curb. She felt a hand on her shoulder, then another on her ankles. Something went around her feet and pulled tight. She panicked when she realized she couldn't move her legs, but they had her hands.

She twisted in their grip, but they pulled her up and onto a stretcher. Meg gave up. What use was there in fighting. Tim had become a monster and was killed. The neighbors were dead. Everyone was dead, and the world was ending. She let the soldiers wrap restraining straps around her so she couldn't move from the stretcher.

Two people picked up the stretcher and Meg felt herself being carried away from the house. Away from Tim's mutilated body.

They lifted her into the back of a truck and Meg smelled the thick scent of diesel exhaust mixed with oiled canvas. A soldier sat down on a bench beside her head and leaned close to her.

"Can you speak, ma'am? Can you tell us your name?"

"Meg," she said through her sobs. "Meg Pratt."

"Meg Pratt," the soldier said to someone else. Meg heard a woman speaking and caught the telltale static click of a two-way radio.

"We're going to get you to safety, ma'am. We're taking you where there's help. Just hold on."

Something inside of Meg switched on. She felt it like a memory crawling up from a long time ago.

"Help," she said.

"What's that, ma'am?" the young soldier asked. Meg felt his hand on her shoulder tense up, and she rolled her head to the side and opened her eyes so she could look at him.

"I'm fine. I'm not infected. It was just my husband. I'm a firefighter; I can help."

The soldier released his grip on her shoulder and

looked her in the eye. Meg felt her tears stop.

"Can you take me into Manhattan? I need to get to my engine's house."

"We'll get you there, ma'am," the soldier said. "Manhattan is the safe zone, at least right now."

The truck gave a jerk and moved down the street, rolling at a good pace. The sounds of other engines told Meg they were probably in a convoy. She heard more gunshots and shouting nearby, and still some of the horrifying shrieks of the monsters. The soldier by her head said something to the other person in the truck and Meg heard the two-way radio again.

"Where's your house?" the soldier asked.

Meg gave her engine number and closed her eyes, trying to relax her breathing and focus on the work ahead. She listened while the soldier told her about the outbreak. It had started in Chicago with an infected person on an airplane. The virus spread to JFK overnight. Queens was being overrun. The Army and Coast Guard were working together to keep the bridges to Manhattan secure.

So far the infection still hadn't spread there, but they expected it would eventually.

Whatever it was, this disease moved faster than anything Meg had ever heard of. With thoughts about Tim trying to force their way into her mind, Meg did her best to keep cool and remember who she was and why she did this job that she loved.

"Because nothing's going to slow me down," she muttered under her breath. One of the soldiers in the truck said something to her, but she didn't reply.

Help was coming to the people of New York City. Help named Meg Pratt.

— 8 —

Jed let his arms relax, but he kept the Glock in front of him, hoping whoever was behind him didn't know he was armed. But what the fuck happened to Chips? Did he go into the wrong apartment? This was his place; Jed knew the door from all the times he'd gone through it when they were in school.

"Easy, *cabrón*," a voice said. Jed didn't recognize it, so he stayed cool. But he wasn't going to go down like a bitch either.

"Yo, I'm a friend of Chips. *Amigo*, you in there? Tell this moth—"

The gun went away from Jed's back and hands grabbed him by the shoulders and yanked him inside. The door slammed shut in front of him and he was spun around by whoever had pulled him in. Jed tried to bring the Glock up, but another hand was on his wrist holding his arm down at his side. He went to look at whoever held his hand, but the man in front of him slapped him once and demanded his attention.

"Look at me, *cabrón*. Just me."

51

Jed looked into the angry face of a man he'd never seen before. The guy's skin was wrinkled like he was a three-pack addict. His narrow brown eyes looked familiar. Like Chips's eyes. Maybe this dude was Chips's uncle or something. He was a lot older than anyone Jed had ever seen around the place. He even had gray hairs mixed in with the jet black stubble on top of his head.

"You a friend of Miguel? The fuck you coming around with a gun in you hand if you his friend?" the old man demanded, holding a little snub nose in Jed's face.

"I'm— I'm Jed. Me and Chip—Miguel, we know each other from back in the day. I was— He gave me the gun."

Jed didn't know how much to let on about why Chips gave him the gun. If this guy was Chips's dad or uncle, he probably knew what Chips was into. Hell, the guy probably got Chips started in the game. But still…

"Okay, *pendejo.* Okay. Tito," the man said now, looking over Jed's shoulder.

Jed felt the Glock being slipped from his grasp and then his hand was let go. Tito, one of Chips' brothers, stepped around from behind Jed and looked him in the eye.

"He's okay, *Tío.* Just some dude Miguel knows from school. I think he's cool."

Tito and the older man traded a few lines in Spanish that Jed couldn't follow. He wanted to interrupt and ask about the zombies and where Chips was at, but they spoke so fast he couldn't figure out where to put his question. Then they stopped and both stared at him.

"Okay," the man said, tucking in his snub nose at the small of his back. "You can stay with us. For now. *Miguel y Memo* coming back soon. They out getting supplies."

"Supplies?" Jed asked, even as he figured the man meant gear they would need for survival. "Because of the zombies. Yeah. Cool."

Tito shared a look with the guy, and Jed wondered if he'd stuck his foot in his own mouth. Then the older man said, "*Sí,* because of the zombies." He smiled when he said the word and that made Jed's skin crawl like it wanted to run out the door and leave him standing there looking like a zombie freak himself.

The three men stood there for a solid minute of awkward damn silence. Jed wanted to take a seat, but the only place to sit was a funky ass sofa up against the wall opposite the door. Tito was standing near it, with Jed's Glock in his hand still. Jed looked at the gun and then at Tito, who just shook his head, like he was saying *Uh-uh, no can do, homie.*

Jed stuck his hands in his pockets and stared around the place, at the shitty carpet and the stained walls, the light fixtures on the ceiling, all full of dead bugs. That's when Jed realized none of the lights were on. He was going to ask about the power being out, but gunfire sounded from the apartment above. Tito and the old man stared at the ceiling with worry or fear dragging their mouths into frowns. The old man put his hand on his snub nose.

Racing footsteps stomped against the floor above. A door slammed open. The footsteps clattered down the concrete balcony and out of earshot.

"The fuck was that?" Jed asked. "Is that—"

The door flew open and someone piled into Jed, knocking him down on his face. Jed tried to get to his feet, but whoever had knocked him down had fallen with him. They were tangled up with a knee in Jed's back and what felt like two sets of arms wrapped around his head. A backpack or some other bag was on Jed's legs, and he had to struggle just to get to his knees under him.

The door slammed shut.

A pair of hands grabbed Jed under the arms and lifted him up. He tried to shrug out of the grip, but whoever it was had him tight. Then he was being spun around, and ended up looking at Chips.

"*Amigo,* you all right, yeah?" Chips asked, pulling Jed in for a quick hug. "Sorry I had to cut out like that. *Tio Rafi* needed some things from his place."

Jed shook it off and gave Chips a nod. His little brother, Memo, was standing next to him. His thick black hair hung down on one side of his face, covering half his eye and cheek. The kid was just a runt when Jed left for the Marines, but he was coming up now, looking more like a man. Jed gave the kid a nod, then asked Chips, "How'd you get out? I was by the door right after you…"

"Back door, homie. *Tio Rafi* lives upstairs. We went up the balcony," Chips said. Then he turned to the older man. "Some of them zombies up in your place, *Tio.* But me and Memo got 'em."

Jed noticed Memo wasn't looking too happy. His upper lip kept curling up, like he wanted to snarl or spit, but was afraid to make any sound at all. The kid was scared, that much was easy to see. But something else was going on with him.

"Yo, everything cool, Memo?" Jed asked.

"Course everything's cool," Chips said before Memo could answer. The kid reached down and grabbed up the backpack that had fallen on Jed's legs. It was heavy, Jed could tell, and the kid had to use both hands to get it up onto his shoulder. Then Memo shook and coughed, nearly dropping the pack. He put a hand up to cover his mouth.

Chips backed up a step and looked at him. Jed did the same and so did Tito and the old man. Then Memo's body bucked, like he'd been kicked in the back. His head whipped back. Jed stepped back another pace right as Memo doubled over. A spray of blood shot out of his mouth, covering Tito's face and the old man's, too. Chips had an arm up and backpedaled into the kitchen.

"Fuck!" Jed screamed.

Tito spun away to Jed's right, stumbling and landing on the couch. He and the old man both wiped at their eyes, but in seconds the wiping turned into scratching. Then both men clawed at their faces as they shook and howled about things Jed couldn't see.

"Get 'em off me, *Tio*! Get 'em off of me, please!" Tito shouted.

The old man screamed in Spanish and swatted at the air around his head. In a heartbeat, he went still, with a look on his bloodied face that told Jed the man was losing his mind. His eyes bugged out and seemed to follow a fly or a mosquito, but Jed didn't see anything buzzing around the room. Memo had gone down on all fours. The backpack landed behind him with a heavy *thud*. Chips had his gun out, but tears streaked down his face as he watched his brothers and uncle twitch and convulse on the floor.

"No, no, no," Chips said, shaking hard and only half-heartedly lifting his gun. Finally he got the muzzle up, but he didn't fire. Jed looked left and right. His Glock was on the couch next to Tito, but Jed wasn't about to go near the guy. Not now. Not with all that blood and shit leaking out of his mouth. Tito tumbled off the couch and wretched. A stream of thick blackish liquid spilled onto the carpet by his face. The old man was shaking again, and grabbing at the air like he was fighting a ghost.

Chips aimed his gun right at Memo then. "I'm sorry, *hermano*. I'm so sorry," Chips said. He looked away as he pulled the trigger. Jed jumped when the gun went off.

The bullet just went into the floor by Memo's hand. Memo reared back and shrieked at Chips, then spun in place to look right at Jed. The kid's face was a mess of pulsing veins and twitching yellow eyes. Blood ran from every hole in his head, and his mouth was already a horrific sucker. Jed could see Memo's teeth crushing together behind his puffy, bloody lips. As he watched, a set of needle-like teeth pushed up from behind his normal ones, and some of those fell out to land on the carpet in a pile of bloody goo.

"The fuck is this? The fu—Chips, man. Your brother's—"

Another gunshot cracked and Memo's face exploded, spraying blood and brains onto the carpet. Jed heaved his guts, adding to the mess. He staggered to the side and tripped over Tito's legs, landing on the couch. His hand found the Glock, but he nearly fumbled it trying to get away from Tito's clutching hands.

A hiss got his attention. The old man was on his stomach now, with his legs bent all wrong, like his joints went backwards. Then his arms clicked and popped and he reared up from the waist, pivoting on the carpet. He went back and forth, first looking at Jed and then at Chips with those sickly yellow eyes and a sucker mouth full of needles.

"Jed, *hermano*. You gotta do it. I can't—"

"Chips, man, this ain't the time to go soft. Not now, man."

The old man shuffled in place and aimed his face in Chips' direction. Jed lifted the Glock and fired, right into the old man's back. Then he put one into Tito who had started whipping his arms and legs up and down, making these crazy popping sounds. Jed finished the job with one to the head for each of the men.

Another gunshot split the air and Jed snapped a hand to his stomach. But he hadn't been shot. He'd just felt it, like it was supposed to happen. But if it wasn't him…

He looked into the kitchen to see Chips sliding down the fridge with his gun stuffed under his chin. Chips' brains covered the freezer door. His arm flopped loose and the gun fell out of his grip to clatter on the kitchen floor. His body followed it and landed with a *thump*.

Jed held a hand over his heart and kept the Glock up and ready as he watched Chips die.

"Stupid motherfucker," Jed said. "Why'd you have to do that, Chips? Why'd you—Shit." Careful to avoid the blood and gore that seemed to cover every surface, Jed went up closer to Chips' body. "Why'd you have to… Shit, man. Shit."

He used a kitchen towel to collect weapons off Tito and the old man. They had their gats stuffed in the back of their pants, and were still face down. The guns didn't seem to have any blood on them, but Jed knew he had to be sure. He lifted Tito's out with the towel and held it up, checking for any blood. When he didn't see any, he tossed the piece away from the bodies to a clean part of the floor. Then he did the same with the uncle's little snub nose. Memo's gat was tucked into his waistband in front, so Jed left it there. He went back to the kitchen and grabbed Chips' gun out of his dead hand. He didn't worry about the blood because he'd seen how the man went out.

You weren't sick, man. You didn't have none of Memo's blood on you. Why'd you have to do it?

Jed found a couple extra mags in Chips' pockets. He emptied one and used the rounds to reload his Glock before he went through the apartment looking for something to carry his gear in. He didn't find anything but funky smelling mattresses in the bedrooms and some old clothes.

He got back to the front room and heard sirens outside. They were far enough away that he didn't worry about them. He knew that something big was going down. If he did run into any 5-0, they'd probably give him a uniform and some extra ammo before they gave him a pair of handcuffs.

Yeah, bullshit. They'd take me down just like always. This here's the Jed show now.

Jed looked at his dead friend and the other dudes.

"Guess maybe you saved yourself some hurt, Chips. I'll see you on the other side, homie."

Jed grabbed up the backpack that Memo had dropped. He hefted it and felt something boxy inside. Jed unzipped the largest pouch. It was full of ammo, boxes of 9mm and some .40 caliber. He stuffed the other pistols into the bag, zipped it up, and put it on. He kept his Glock in his hand. He'd have to get a holster for it soon.

He was about to leave when he thought about the money in his pocket. Jed went back and rifled through Chips's pants. He came up with a thick wad that he stuffed in his pocket, rolled up tight. It wasn't a bank roll, but it was a start. If he played it right, he could probably get his own place when it was all over.

Finally stop living in grandma's house.

Jed went to the door and lifted his gun. He opened the door slowly and looked outside. A boy and girl sat like hunting cats on the other side of the pool area. The girl chewed on a human arm that had been torn off at the elbow. The boy seemed to be thinking about doing the same thing and kept dancing closer to the girl, but she swiped at him with her claws and he backed away. Jed gasped and they turned to look at him and hissed. Then the girl shrieked and they both charged, leaping around the ends of the pool like wild beasts. Jed fired three quick shots that went into the ground. He aimed better and fired again. The girl went down with two holes in her stomach and half her face missing. The boy nearly got to Jed before he pivoted left and fired his last few rounds. They hit the kid right in the chest. He went down and slammed face first into the front stoop.

— 9 —

The truck rumbled under Meg's back, picking up speed at times, lurching and jerking at others.

"Can you let me up now?" Meg asked the soldier whose foot was right by her ear. She was tired of worrying if he was going to suddenly kick her the next time the truck lurched. The other soldier, the woman, made *an uh-uh* sound, but the first soldier leaned down and looked Meg in the eyes. She'd stopped crying. Tim was dead, gone and never to return. Whatever was happening, it was huge, and he wasn't the only husband who was lost. Wives were probably dying. And children, no doubt.

"People are going to need my help when we get to the house. I can help faster if I don't have to unwind the knots in my arms and legs first."

"Okay, ma'am," the soldier said. He set his gun aside, laying it on the bench beside him. Then Meg felt the other soldier move from her bench. Hands went to the straps on Meg's arms and ankles. Finally she could move

61

again and slowly stretched her limbs as the truck rumbled on. By the time they pulled up in front of her station house, Meg felt limber and warm and ready to get to work.

The soldiers motioned for her to wait while they looked out the back of the truck. Meg could see another truck behind them with two soldiers in the cab. Some hand signals went back and forth and the female soldier gave Meg the okay to get out. The woman shifted to sit on the bench again, holding her gun up and looking at the surrounding buildings like a monster might drop from them at any moment. The soldier's tight features and grim posture told Meg this was more serious than she'd imagined.

"What's happening? What are they?" she asked.

The woman grunted again, but the man answered from behind Meg. He'd moved to sit on the opposite bench.

"Some kind of monsters. We don't know, ma'am. But— Don't let 'em bite you or get any of their blood on you. And if you see anyone get bit, do 'em a favor."

"A favor—" Meg started to say, but then realized what the soldier meant. She looked back and forth at them for a moment, taking in the man's young features. He looked scared, she could tell, but not ready to give up. The woman wasn't much older than him, but something had aged her recently. Meg had seen the look before, on people who had been there on 9/11.

"Thank you," Meg said. She hopped down from the truck, catching the eyes of the soldiers in the truck cab behind them. One of them raised a hand and Meg waved back. She said, "Good luck," turned, and said the same to the man and woman who had rescued her.

***

Meg stepped into the chief's office, closed the door behind her and turned the deadbolt. The street outside had been quiet, but the house seemed deserted. The chief's desk to her right was a scattered mess of papers and pens. Just like it always was. His coffee cup was upended and a brown ring on his desk blotter showed where it used to sit.

In front of Meg, the secretary's desk sat quiet and empty, behind the low reception counter.

Nobody's here? Why did they leave the door unlocked?

She tensed when she heard a soft scraping sound from the app floor. Meg stepped around the chief's desk. Through the doorway into the app floor, she saw Eric and Rex coming up the basement stairs carrying cots. They had their turnout pants on and boots. The echo of the receding military truck engines faded away outside as Meg stepped onto the floor.

"Meg!" Eric shouted when she came in. He ran to her and held her tight for a moment, and she returned the embrace. Tears sprang to her eyes again when she realized how afraid she'd been that she'd never see him or the house again.

"It's okay," she said, pulling in a sob as they stepped apart. Rex came up to them.

"Good to see you again, Meg," the big man said and held his arms out like he'd hug her. Meg gave him a quick embrace, slapping him on the back and stepping away just as fast. "Glad you made it," Rex said, patting his hands on his pants. "We're getting the triage set up. Dispatch called the engine and ladder out about an hour ago. Then it was call after call. Non-stop. But…"

Meg looked at Eric. His face went into a tight frown. "The engine and ladder have been gone too long. I'm afraid we might be on our own here."

"What do you mean?" Meg asked. "The streets are almost empty. Can't they get back?"

Rex and Eric traded a look that threatened to put Meg back on the ground, curled up and in terror. But she let her anger at the situation get the upper hand.

"If we've lost them, and we're all that's left, then we'd better get to work."

Eric gave her a smile and went the basement stairs. "I'll get more cots. We'll probably need them."

"We should be safe in here," Rex said, still standing there like he was waiting for something from Meg.

"I'm not worried about us, Rex," she said.

A banging on the shutter doors froze them in place. Eric had just come up from the basement with a folded cot under each arm.

"What's that?" he asked.

The banging repeated, moving along the shutters, in the direction of the entrance. Meg went to the doorway to the chief's office and looked at the glass front door. A man leaned up against the door, holding someone close to him. The man looked scared, and clearly in need of help. But he wasn't a monster.

Not yet anyway.

Lifting an axe from the wall beside her, Meg stepped into the office, staying behind the front counter. The man shouted and his muffled voice came through the window.

"We need help! There's a whole line of us out here. The Army left without us and you guys weren't coming. We need— We need help."

Meg nodded at him and tried to smile. "Okay," she shouted back. We'll help you."

The man sagged against the door with what looked like relief, and Meg nodded at him. She was going to ask if anybody outside had been infected, but her eyes were drawn to the secretary's desk behind the counter. The phone was lit up with every line flashing.

"Eric!" she called back to him. "The phone's going crazy. Why isn't it ringing?"

"We turned off the ringer," Rex said from the doorway behind her. "It wouldn't stop, and we couldn't go anywhere anyway. The Army guys said we had to stay here in case people started coming to us. Looks like they have."

Meg looked up at the door again. The man was still there, holding his arm around whoever he'd brought with him. It looked like it might be a young girl. Meg could see other people milling around, huddled together, some looking like they were about to fall over and others turning their heads left and right like scared rabbits. It was a big group, at least twenty or more.

The man in front of the door clutched an arm around his companion, and she hung onto him tightly. Maybe it was his daughter? Meg thought she could see long blonde hair under a coat that was covering the person's head and shoulders. Rex was still in the doorway behind her.

"Rex, will you—"

In that instant, Meg felt the world slide out from under her feet. Dizziness whipped her head to the side and she fell against the counter. She only kept hold of her axe because she had the head hooked over the edge of the counter.

Outside the door, the crowd of people screamed and ran in different directions. The man by the window stayed put. And he changed. His eyes grew a sickly yellow. Blood leaked from them and from his nose, like he'd just gone ten rounds with a prize fighter. The person next to him, under the coat, shook and staggered back a step, so that she was out of view for a moment.

Then the person stepped back into view. It had been a woman once, maybe a girl, but not anymore. A monstrous face of pale white flesh pressed up against the window. The woman's skin was criss-crossed with scratches and thick blue veins, and her mouth had grown into a bulbous sucker, just like Tim's had. Needle-like teeth stuck out from between the puffy, blood-stained lips.

The infected man fell backwards, giving the monster room to fill the window. The creature reared its head back and then slammed it forward, splitting the glass into shards that fell out of the frame. She did it again, not even noticing when slivers of glass sliced into her cheeks and forehead. The creature let out a horrifying shriek.

— 10 —

Elmhurst, Queens

Jed juked down an alley between two apartment blocks, moving away from the screams and looking for a hiding place at every turn. He had to get to his grandma's place. It was the only safe spot he could think of, and he still had a couple doses of cotton tucked away under his mattress.

Small crowds ran down the street with cops and soldiers around them. Jed hid from them all. He knew the cops would take him down for what he had in his backpack. Safety in numbers was one thing, but right now Jed was only thinking about *Number One*.

After what felt like an hour of playing cat and mouse with the cops and all the screaming people running around the city, Jed was finally near his grandma's place. Up ahead, the low balcony hung from the side of the apartment building. The fire escape was down. Jed went for it, climbed up quiet, and put his hand under his shirt to lift the Glock when he got to the top. He was careful not to touch the trigger.

Learned that lesson like a damn fool. But I learned it.

The balcony was off the kitchen of his grandma's apartment. Jed looked through the glass door. It looked cool inside, nothing crazy like he'd seen in them places back near where Chips lived. The furniture was all where it was supposed to be, and he didn't see any blood. The pictures were still on the wall above his grandma's pink sofa. His own smiling face stared back at him from the biggest picture. He'd been eight years old when it was taken, hanging out on the subway with his grandpa right after his dad died and his mom sent him up to New York.

Jed tried the door. It was open, and right away he knew something was wrong. His grandma never left the doors unlocked. He slid the door open slowly. The place smelled like shit. Jed put a hand up over his nose, waited, and listened. He kept the Glock up and ready.

Weapon at the ready. Clear the room and move on.

Jed poked his gun around the corner of the door, aiming at the kitchen. He kept his finger alongside the trigger, just not on it. A trickle of sweat ran down his arm under his shirt sleeve and tickled his wrist. He had to slap his other hand around the Glock to keep from dropping the thing. A wave of funky stink came to his nose and he gagged, but he kept his stomach down. He gave a quick shake of his head and let some of that bullshit from the suck go through his mind, get him pumped like the drills told him it would back in Boot.

He poked his head into the place.

The lights were all off, but the sun was sneaking down into the alley and lighting everything up. Jed could see the kitchen better now. There was a frying pan on the stove, all covered in dried egg or something disgusting and yellow. Flied buzzed over the mess and around the sink.

Jed gagged hard when he checked the sink and threw up a little in his mouth. He spit it out and wiped his mouth on his sleeve.

The sink was full of some funky shit, like chewed up sausage, with dried blood all over it.

He flinched when he heard a clicking sound, like someone drawing back the bolt on a weapon. The sound came from down the hallway off the room with the sofa. Jed spun around to see his grandma come into the room on all fours. She was fucked up, turned into one of the zombies, and Jed felt his guts try to let go in his pants. He kept it in, but backed up until he was leaning against the sink. His grandma crawled forward on her stomach, but her arms and legs were all crazy. She moved like some kind of spider. Blood leaked out of her eyes and everything. And her eyes—

It was like some kind of monster movie. His grandma's eyes were yellow slits now.

Jed reared back as she let out a loud hiss. He'd thought she was just making a face at first, but now he could see what happened to her mouth. It was like a suction cup, all round and with a bunch of sharp ass teeth like little pins inside.

Jed watched, with his throat closing up, as his grandma clamped onto her own arm and chewed out a chunk of flesh. Lifting the Glock, Jed said, "I'm sorry, Grandma. Sorry—" He squeezed the trigger, but nothing happened. His grandma twitched her head at him and shrieked so loud he almost had to drop the gun so he could cover his ears.

His grandma came at him, jumped forward and landed between him and the glass door. Jed racked the slide and fired. His shots went wide, but he corrected his aim, putting rounds into his grandma's chest and face. She went down in a heap. Her brains blew out the back of her head. Jed heaved again, coughing up whatever was left in his stomach as he staggered past her body. He kept the Glock on her as he stepped out the balcony door. He looked up the ladder and thought about going higher, safer. Then he remembered the one thing his squad leader said that felt helpful.

"You don't go up to get safe. Going up leaves you only one way out. And that's down."

Jed went down the fire escape and ran. He made it to the end of the alley before he heard more screams behind him, and some other sounds. Shrieking, like some wild animal shit, and then the heavy *chop-chop-chop* of a Ma deuce from down at the end of the alley. The unmistakable sound of boots on pavement echoed down the alley then, and for the first time in a long time, Jed smiled at the thought of being around the military again.

Four army dudes came running down the alley, all with M4s and covered in battle rattle. One of them called up to. "You okay up there? Have you contacted any infected?"

Jed looked at himself all over, checked his pants and sleeves. He was clean.

"I'm good. No blood, man. I'ma come down. Okay?"

"Okay, but hands where I can see 'em. Gotta know you're friendly."

Jed switched the Glock to his other hand so he could hold it by the slide and with his fingers away from the trigger. He held the gun over his head and slowly went down the ladder, one foot down, then the other. A team of soldiers waited at the bottom, eyes out on the alleyway and all the balconies above them.

Shit, if Grandma was infected…

"We gotta move, Sarge," one of the soldiers said.

Jed looked up, following the soldier's line of sight. Three of the monsters crawled down the side of the building, lips all puckered and sucking together like leeches out for blood. Their arms and legs bent at weird angles and their joints popped and clicked.

"Go men. Go!" the sergeant yelled. He fired off a burst at the lowest of the monsters and it came down, falling like a dead bat to land in a messy heap. Its flailing arms banged off a balcony railing on the way down.

The other soldiers bailed with their sergeant on their heels.

Jed thought about trying to cap one of the monsters on the wall, but two more emerged from a window on the top floor. They jumped from the window and landed on the building across the alley. Now four of them, with their greasy looking white flesh and bloody yellow eyes, crawled down at him, and from both sides.

"C'mon!" the sergeant yelled at Jed from the end of the alley.

Finally Jed's feet got the message his brain was trying to send, and he ran like hell after the soldiers. They'd made it to a Humvee at the end of the alley and were piling inside. The top gunner swiveled his Ma deuce and opened up on the creatures tearing down the walls after Jed. Bits of brick peppered down on Jed's head as he ran, fearing any second that one of the shrieking horrors behind him would land on him and clamp down on his neck.

— 11 —

Upper East Side, Manhattan

Meg lifted her axe from the counter edge and sprang forward, putting a foot on the desk and climbing over the counter. She swung the axe up and brought it down just as the monster was thrusting its face through the shattered window.

The axe split the creature's skull and splattered gore onto the floor at Meg's feet. Meg took a stance away from the bloody mess on the floor and carefully removed her axe so she wouldn't spatter any blood on herself. She had to be ready for the man to try and break in. But she only heard the screams of people running away outside. The corpse of the one she'd killed hung half in the window, with clawed hands reaching toward the floor as if to scoop up the brains and blood.

She could hear Rex almost whimpering behind her. "Where is it? The other one. Where is it?" he said.

"Not here, genius," Meg said, finally fed up with the bigger man's candy-assing. "Eric! Are you okay?"

"Yeah," he said, coming up behind Rex. He had a

nozzle under one arm and the hose held around his waist with the other hand. "Let's put up a barrier or something. We'll have to hold them off from the app floor."

"What if people come in and need help?" Rex asked.

Meg curled her lip up and looked at him like he was an idiot. "If they need help, we have to make sure they're not infected first."

"What if they are?"

"If they are, we can't help them."

"She's right," Eric said, still eyeing the body hanging through the window. "If anybody comes around with blood on them, they're already lost. We're probably on our own."

They retreated into the app floor and shoved a folding table and some trash barrels into the doorway. It wouldn't hold anything bigger than a squirrel, and Meg knew it. But it was all they could do for now. The engine and truck were gone, making the floor just one big open space with gear and now cots piled up around the edges.

Eric held the hose on the door while Rex and Meg suited up in their full turnout gear, including face shields. Once she had her gloves on, Meg held the hose so Eric could get suited up. When he was ready, she passed the hose back and retrieved her axe, finding comfort in the familiar weight of the…*weapon*.

"Eric, keep the hose aimed at the door. Rex, let's get some better barricades set up. We can use the dirty lockers for starters.

Without waiting for a reply, Meg marched toward the lockers at the back of the floor. They weren't secured to the wall, so they could be shoved into place to block the open doorway. They would only cover the bottom two thirds of the opening, but it would create a funnel for the things to get through, and that might give them a chance at survival until help arrived.

Meg hesitated before she set her axe down. She threw a look over her shoulder at the heavy shutters that shielded them from whatever was happening outside.

They were safe. Only for now, maybe, but still. They were safe.

Rex hadn't moved. Eric aimed the hose at the doorway to the chief's office.

"Rex," Meg said. "Let's go."

The big man shuffled toward her, looking back over his shoulder every few steps.

"They're not inside, Rex. And if they get inside, Eric has the hose. He'll keep them from getting to us while we move this." Meg slapped a hand against the lockers and the metallic *clank* echoed. Rex jumped. Then he seemed to shake off whatever was eating at him and bent to help push the bank of lockers across the floor.

The metal case squeaked, creaked, and groaned as they shoved it together. Meg pushed from the top and Rex squatted down to use the power in his thick legs, shoving from the base of the lockers. A loud shriek startled them and they halted their progress, both of them looking to Eric to see if he'd heard it.

He had. His face was slack when he said, "That was you guys. The locker scraped on the floor."

Meg and Rex leaned back to push the locker again. But Meg screamed a warning instead.

The man from before was back, and he'd fully changed. He was no longer a man, just a monster hanging upside down from the ceiling in the chief's office. Its ghastly white face stuck through the doorway. The creature's bloody yellowed eyes were fixed on Meg and Rex. Then it flicked its predatory gaze to Eric and opened its sucker mouth. The thing let out a shriek that nearly split Meg's eardrums.

Eric aimed the hose up and opened the valve, releasing a torrent straight into the thing's sucker mouth. The creature shrieked and flew backwards from the spray, landing out of sight in the entry office. Eric kept up the spray and Meg thought she heard the sound of the monster scrabbling on the floor or climbing the walls.

"The axe, Meg! Help!" Eric shouted over the rush of water.

Meg reeled away from the lockers, leaving Rex to the task on his own. It was something simple, something he could be good at and that would keep him out of her way. She snapped up her axe from where they'd started pushing the locker, and cursed herself for ever leaving it behind to begin with. In a second, Meg was past Rex and standing beside Eric, holding her axe at the ready.

The monster was pinned to the far wall of the chief's office, behind the secretary's desk. The jet of water crushed into its chest. Its arms flailed and its head whipped side to side, with a thick tongue snaking out of its sucker mouth. Shrieks echoed around the app floor like something out of a carnival horror show.

Meg stepped to the side, avoiding the flow of water, and brought her axe up over her head. She kicked the trash barrels aside at the doorway and waited for them to roll clear before she shoved the folding table with her foot. It slid a foot or so, but got hung up on the door jamb. Rex appeared on the other side and yanked it out of the way. When the path was clear, Meg slipped around the jet of water and into the chief's office. She stepped forward and sliced down in a single motion, burying the blade in the monster's skull just as she'd done with the first one.

Eric kept the hose on it until its arms stopped clawing at the air and it drooped against the wall. Meg backed away as Eric turned the flow off. The wet *slop slop* of Meg's boots on the floor almost mimicked the sound of the creatures as they smacked their puffy lips together.

"We'd better see if the other people are still outside," Eric said, keeping the hose up and at the ready.

Meg agreed and, with her axe in one hand, went to the shutter doors. She climbed up on one door and looked through the window. Outside, the street seemed quiet and deserted, about as unusual and haunting a sight as Meg had ever seen.

"I never thought I'd see what New York looks like without all the people in it."

Then Meg spotted them, the crowd from before. They shuffled out of their hiding places in alleys and doorways, like a crew of homeless people coming for the dinner bell.

Rex was at the shutters. He only had to stand on tip toe to see out the window.

"We should help—"

"We should wait to see if any of them are infected first," Meg said.

A siren whined from the up the street and Meg felt her mood lift instantly. "The engine's back!"

Eric kept the hose up, but he backed away, across the floor. Meg stepped down and moved to open the shutters. Rex put a hand up and shouted for her to stop.

"I don't think it's them," he said. His voice shook as he continued, "It's not— It's not them."

Meg heard a screech of metal on metal, and the heavy thunk of a vehicle colliding with another, and then another thud. She lifted herself up to look through the window, fearing what she would see. The engine had stopped just before making the turn that would aim its rear at the station so they could back in. They'd swiped two cars parked on the street and had smashed head on into another as they rounded the corner.

"What're they doing?" Meg wondered aloud. The cab of the engine shook. Blood sprayed out the side window, and then more of it came in a gout. Rex whimpered beside her as Meg watched in horror while their friends were killed. It was over in less than a minute, and Meg, Eric, and Rex stayed silent for longer than that, just staring into the emptiness around them. Meg wanted to find a way out, some way to leave the city, to go somewhere safe. If she'd listened to Tim…

We'd both be dead. We couldn't have escaped.

Meg looked out the shutter windows again. She tried to move her attention away from the remains of their crew, now emerging from the truck and tumbling to the pavement, kicking and clawing at the air. Then the first of them rose as an infected creature. Meg didn't want to look, but she had to watch.

She could see their bodies changing as they moved. She recognized faces in the instant before eyes yellowed and blood ran in rivulets down pale white cheeks. Before mouths popped open in a horrific O with rows of sharp needles where teeth had once been.

Meg's friends died out there on the street, only to be

reborn as monsters. The creatures crawled along the street with joints audibly cracking as they moved, like freakish spiders—

"The people!" Eric shouted from behind her. Meg snapped her gaze to the small crowd that had been hiding in the street outside. They had all grouped together and shuffled backwards, away from the transforming firefighters. Rex was still useless, watching it all unfold through the window and doing nothing to stop it.

Without a second thought, Meg rushed for the dirty lockers they'd been shoving along the floor. She snatched a turnout jacket and sped back to the chief's office, kicking the trash barrels clear out of the way this time. At the front door, she yelled for the people to come her way. She put her axe against the wall and used the jacket to cover the dead thing hanging through the window. With the jacket as a protective cover, Meg grabbed the body and heaved it over backwards.

An older black woman outside ran up and dragged the corpse off to the side.

"Don't get any blood on you!" Meg shouted, reaching for her axe in the same motion. The woman had a look on her face that said she was ready for whatever was coming. She held up her hands to show she was wearing yellow latex gloves.

"It ain't much, but it helps."

Meg gave her a look of relief as together they opened the door fully. The woman waved her gloved hands to usher everyone into the house. The group was mostly women with a few children, but a couple of men were at the back.

Meg hefted her axe as she went outside with the

survivors, holding the door open and waving the people forward. They were all colors and ages and shapes. People from everywhere in the city, it seemed. She looked closely and tried to make eye contact with each of them as they came in. Some of them smiled, and Meg did her best to smile back. But she wasn't looking at them as people yet.

They all look clean. For now.

A shriek tore Meg's attention from the group for a moment, and she watched as a former friend of hers, now a monster, leaped from atop a car to tackle a man at the back of the line. With a shout, Meg ran forward, past the line of survivors making their way into the house. She lifted her axe as she ran and swung with all her strength, burying the axe head in the monster's back just as it lowered its mouth to feed on the man it had brought down.

— 12 —

Elmhurst, Queens

The sun was climbing higher by the time Jed and the soldiers connected up with the military's main element at Newtown High over in Elmhurst. Jed remembered lying in the middle of the track when him and Chips were stoned late at night, and sometimes running laps on it during the day when they *did* show up for gym class. Now the track and ball fields were a motor pool and command point. They'd come in with Humvees and some old open-bed trucks, and even a Bradley. Tents were going up in between lines of vehicles, and patrols of twos and threes walked the fence line with their weapons up and at the ready.

"Fuck me," Jed said.

"Yeah, man," said one of the soldiers next to him. "Shit's on with a vengeance."

"All this for some zombies?"

The soldier looked at Jed like he was crazy. "They ain't zombies, brother. I don't know who told you that, but— Believe it. Fuckin' monsters out there. Zombies would be easy as the BRM range, all slow and shit. You'd hit 'em at two hundred meters, no problem. These fuckers, man you got lucky back there. I seen just two of them tear into a whole squad. They took out the SAW gunner first, like they knew he was the big threat. I swear. They ain't zombies. Zombies don't think or plan their attack."

Jed's eyes went wide at that and he kept quiet for the rest of the ride. Finally, they pulled up beside an idling Humvee and the sergeant by the tailgate told everyone to dismount. The soldiers hopped off and moved out to the ball fields where a platoon was lining up in formation. Jed jumped down with the soldier who'd talked to him. The guy gave him a nod and jogged off to join the formation. Jed figured he should follow, but another NCO, some thin Asian dude, came around the truck and put a hand on Jed's arm, holding him back.

"You got a name there, *Hardcore?*"

"Jed. I mean— Welch, Sergeant. My name's Welch. Private Welch, USMC."

The guy blinked once, and stared at Jed like he'd spoken a foreign language. He didn't believe him. Jed could tell. But it was the only play he had right now.

"Marines are out in the field mopping up. What's with the civvie gear and the gat stuffed in your pants?"

The sergeant was at least an E-6. Jed didn't know Army rank that well, but he knew authority when he heard it, no matter how many stripes it had on.

"I'm home from Iraq, Sergeant. Just got back. I was hit—"

"Uh-huh. How about you hand over the gat and we talk to the First Sergeant about connecting you with your actual."

Jed had to resist the urge to pull the Glock on the

man. He'd be taken out in two seconds if he tried anything. But he wasn't going to give up his gat. Not that easy.

"I have more in my pack, Sergeant. All from home. I figured they could be useful with the zombies—"

The sergeant busted out laughing but pulled it back in just as fast. He gave Jed a hard stare and jerked his chin up, motioning for Jed to get moving. "Let's go, Hardcore Jed Welch. You and your sack full of guns. First Sergeant's tent is that way."

Jed turned and walked toward the tent across the ball field. He could feel the NCO behind him, and heard the man's battle rattle shift as he lifted his weapon up to carry it at the ready.

Fuck. Fuck, fuck, fuck.

If it went the way he knew it would, Jed was about to lose his Glock and all his ammo, plus any chance he had of getting away alive. They'd put him back with some fucking Marine unit and he'd be back in the suck like he'd never left. What the fuck was he gonna do?

The tent flap up ahead flicked aside and a man stepped out wearing a clean ACU. Jed looked at the other soldiers he could see and realized they all had brand new gear on. The more he thought about it, the more Jed knew that none of these dudes had seen combat. None of 'em, except for maybe the NCO behind him. He had an M4. But all the other guys he'd seen were carrying M16s.

They got up to the First Sergeant and the NCO behind Jed told him to stop. Without thinking, Jed felt his arms moving so his hands snapped up at the small of his back. His legs straightened about shoulder-width apart and he stared straight ahead, holding his chin level.

"First Sergeant Oguein," the NCO said from behind him. "This man here claims to be a Marine, just home from Iraq. Says he was hit, but I don't—"

"What's your name, son?" the First Sergeant asked Jed, looking him right in the eye. The man had black eyes, and a thin mustache. He stood a little shorter than Jed and was heavier around the middle.

"Private Welch, First Sergeant," Jed said. "I was with—"

"You're with the 401st Civil Affairs now, Private Welch. Sergeant Boon will take you to the Quartermaster for your ACUs and then to the armory for a weapon. You can keep your sidearm. Sergeant Boon, make sure he gets holster for it. We don't need any AD injuries."

"Yes, First Sergeant."

Jed felt a hand on his shoulder, prodding him to move. He relaxed his posture and fell into step beside the NCO as they left the First Sergeant's presence.

"That was good, man. Real good," Sergeant Boon said.

Jed didn't want to say anything, but he knew he should. So he grunted the universal term that every Marine knows and says more than a hundred times a day.

"'Rah, Sergeant."

"Yeah," Sergeant Boon said. "Real good."

Jed could tell the man didn't like him and didn't trust him. But who the fuck cared. He wasn't going back to the suck. He could probably count on getting through this shit okay.

Sergeant Boon led him to a tent on the other side of the ball fields. Trucks and Humvees kept circling around the track and pulling into a formation like they were getting ready to convoy into the neighborhoods.

Inside the Quartermaster's tent, Sergeant Boon hung off to the side while Jed got his new uniform. The Quartermaster was a short white dude with red peachfuzz on his top lip and more pimples than Jed had ever seen on anyone's face before. Guy looked like fucking Freddy Krueger. He passed over a pile of clothing and lifted a pair of boots up from a box. The zit-faced guy looked at Jed like he was just some green recruit off the block.

"You a 10 or 10-wide?" he asked, holding out the uniform.

"Yeah," Jed said, accepting the camouflage pants and shirt. "10-wide."

"Yeah?" the dude asked, pushing the boots at Jed. "Your recruiter tell you to say that?"

Jed almost shot back at the dude about how fucked up his face was, but then he noticed the two stripes on the guy's chest tab.

"Yes, Corporal. I mean, no, Corporal," he said, moving into parade rest again with one arm behind his back and the other tucked against his side holding the uniform. He stood sharp, but not as sharp as when he was talking to the First Sergeant.

"Get dressed, Hardcore Jed Welch," Sergeant Boon said. "You got one minute."

Jed mumbled *Rah* this time, and nodded without looking at Sergeant Boon or Corporal McZits. He dropped his pack and stripped out of his clothes in a hurry, making sure to keep his left side exposed and lifting his arm so he could show off his *battle scar* to Sergeant Boon.

If the guy saw it, he either wasn't impressed or decided Jed was all right after all and just didn't want to say anything. Jed could almost feel the hatred coming off both of them as carefully lifted his Glock out of his waistband and laid it on top of his backpack on the ground. Then he kicked off his work boots, dropped his pants, and slipped into the ACU like it was a second skin.

Sergeant Boon coughed once, but didn't say anything while Jed finished putting on his clothes. Corporal McZits dropped a full LBE beside Jed's backpack and went back to getting uniforms and boots stacked up on a set of shelves at the back of the tent. When Jed finished tying on his boots, he picked up the harness and slid into it, clicking the belt clasps and checking the straps to make sure they fit tight enough. Then he came to attention. Sergeant Boon chuckled but gave him a nod that said he felt better about Jed now.

"Let's go, Welch. Armory time. Bring your gat and the pack."

Jed bent down and retrieved his Glock. He slung the pack over one shoulder and carried the pistol at his side with his fingers wrapped around the trigger guard.

At the armory tent, Sergeant Boon had Jed sign for an M16A2 and turn in his pack with the other guns. He got a holster and a box of 9mm ammo for the Glock, plus six more boxes for the M16.

"You can load up on the truck, Welch," Sergeant Boon said. "We move out in fifteen."

"Sergeant?" Jed asked, feeling less sure than he did before.

"Truck, Welch. The one outside, behind this tent. We have two platoons of National Guard here. They just got home last month. You can share war stories and compare scars."

Jed didn't miss the way Sergeant Boon's mouth went from a frown to a shit-eating grin as he said the last few words. He nodded at Sergeant Boon and waited for the guy to give him the signal to leave. All he got was a wrinkled up sneer.

Outside the armory tent, Jed followed a line of soldiers marching to a truck that had just begun rumbling as the driver turned over the engine. A gust of diesel exhaust hit Jed's mouth and he coughed, nearly gagging on the stink. He fucking hated military trucks, and the planes. They had to be designed by some motherfucker who got off making dudes sick before they even got in the damn things.

The line of soldiers in front of Jed came to a stop behind the truck. Jed fell in with them, at ease, looking at the line of uniforms like a bunch of trees all standing ready to get chopped down. Jed looked at his own uniform and remembered the money he had stuffed in his pants pocket.

"Fu—"

"Shut it down, Private," the man next to him said. He was a black guy, and younger than Jed by maybe a few years. He had corporal stripes on his uniform, though, and he looked hard. Jed knew some rough dudes growing up, but this guy looked like a piece of steel got shoved up his ass and all it did was make him want more.

An NCO came up from around the truck and called them to attention. An LT showed up on the heels of the NCO. The officer gave his name, but Jed wasn't listening. He couldn't pay attention to anything the dude said because the shrieks and screams out in the neighborhoods started up right as the LT opened his mouth. Jed caught something about *57ᵗʰ Avenue*, and *Queens Boulevard.*

Then it was everybody jumping through his own asshole, climbing into the truck. Someone yelled about having weapons up and out at the ready. Jed stuck his M16 over the side of the truck and scanned the area around them. All he could see were more trucks and soldiers running all over the fucking place. He heard screams and shouts echoing around the ball fields. Jed could swear he heard a Ma deuce busting out rounds from the other side of the fields.

The truck moved and lurched, making Jed sway. He'd knelt on the bench with one knee and kept the other foot on the truck bed behind him for support. The corporal was to Jed's left and gave him a look. Jed ignored it and went back to looking out for the enemy. Whoever or whatever was out there, he had a real weapon now. It was shaking in his hands, and he tried to hide it so the other dudes wouldn't see. He closed his eyes for a second and thought about Iraq, and the only patrol he'd ever done. His eyes snapped open and he knew he'd make it out of this okay. He held the rifle like it was the only thing keeping him alive, because that's exactly what it was.

He'd make it out okay. He'd get back, even if some of these other dudes didn't, and even if he had to take one or two of them out, like Chips' brothers and their uncle. That's what Jed would do to save his own skin, and that's what he would always do.

Jed was gonna make it.

— 13 —

Meg wrenched the axe out of the monster's back and turned just in time to swing at another one. She didn't recognize who it had been before, so it hurt only a little less when the axe head sank into the man's chest. Meg searched the street for more of the monsters, but she didn't see any. She heard them, though, and the screams they caused as they tore through storefronts and apartments nearby.

Eric was shouting at her to come back. Meg spared one last look at the dying city around her before she joined the line of survivors going into the house. She wiped at the blood and gore that coated her jacket front and went to brush her face shield when her hand stopped in mid air.

What if I'm infected?

"Eric!" she screamed at him as the last of the survivors, the only man left in the group, made it to the door. But Eric was already back inside somewhere, out of earshot. The male survivor was at the door, holding it open for Meg. The broken window in the door looked like an angry mouth full of jagged teeth ready to rip her skin to shreds.

"Are you coming?" the man asked her. He had dirt on his face, covering one side of his forehead and one cheek.

"Is that—" Meg started to ask, just as the man shook and his hands began to clutch at the air. His mouth opened and he let out a howl of pain as he fell to his knees and spasmed on the pavement. His arms and legs flailed and his screams forced an echo of terror into Meg's ears. Still she ran toward him.

"Help me! I can't *see* them! They're *everywhere*! *Help*!"

Meg sank her axe into his skull, hearing the fatal crack of bone and feeling the blade crush through to the pavement. The man's body twitched and went still.

Meg pulled her axe free and used the handle to push her face shield up. She spit to the side, over and over again, fearing she'd got even a drop of infected blood into her mouth somehow. She couldn't shake the feeling that she'd swallowed some and would become a monster herself at any moment.

"Meg?" Rex said from the doorway. "Are you hurt? Did he bite you?"

Staring at Rex, Meg waited. She breathed deep and listened to her heart beat, the blood rushing in her ears, and the sounds of violence cascading around the city in every direction.

You're okay. You're good.

She knew she was okay. It was just her involuntary reflex.

Contaminated bodily fluids. You're fine. You're covered up.

"I'm fine, Rex," she said, dropping her shield into

place and stepping forward. Rex left the doorway so she could come into the house.

Rex had gone back to the app floor where Eric was setting up the survivors on the cots.

"Eric," Meg said. "We need to wash out the chief's office."

He nodded and brought the hose over. While Meg held the broken door open, Eric sent a torrent of water into the office space, pushing as much blood and mess as he could out into the street. Papers and pens, the phone, the chief's mug. All of it went out into the street.

It wasn't anything close to real decontamination, but it would have to do. As a last step, Meg braced herself in the doorway while Eric sprayed her down, cleaning off the spatters of blood that decorated her jacket, trousers, and boots.

Back inside, Rex and Eric performed a quick triage of the survivors, sending anyone with blood on their clothing anywhere to join Meg.

To the survivors, Meg said, "We need to shower. Get cleaned off. If you were outside, and you're not hurt, come with me. We need to decontaminate ourselves."

She shivered when she thought about the stinging sensation that would come from using the disinfecting soaps they had, but it was necessary. Even one droplet of infected blood in the wrong place could mean disaster for everyone.

Nothing's going to slow you down, Meg. Nothing at all.

Rex finished shoving the dirty lockers in front of the doorway to the chief's office while a line of five women and four children joined Meg at the stairs. The others, close to a dozen women of all ages and colors, huddled together at the back of the floor. Only one woman wearing a headscarf stayed near the cots, holding her baby close to her body. Meg could tell the woman was uncomfortable about the situation. Eric seemed to sense it, and with the firehose in his hands again, he approached the woman, staying a few steps back.

"Ma'am? Have you or your child come into contact with anybody who was infected? Have you touched—"

"Yes," the woman almost shouted in reply before she broke into sobs.

"Ma'am, did—Was it someone who was infected? Did you get any blood on you?"

"No. But my husband was dead. I—I touched him," the woman said, turning tear-stained eyes to Eric, then looking directly at Meg, as if she believed Meg could somehow help her. "I knew I should not, but—There is nowhere I can go to purify my body."

Meg felt her heart clench inside. Tim had given up most of his traditional beliefs before they met, but he was just as obsessive about keeping clean as Meg was.

And he still performed a ritual bath after—

Thoughts of their life together ruined any chance Meg had of keeping her own calm. She felt the tears flowing down her cheeks as she watched the Muslim woman struggling with her own suffering.

"We have two showers upstairs," Meg said. Then, to Eric and Rex, she asked, "Have any of the guys used it yet?"

Both men shook their heads, and Meg nodded her thanks before she turned to the Muslim woman again.

"I cleaned the engineer's bathroom at the end of my last shift, and nobody's used it since. It's the best we can do for a woman's bathroom, and I'm the only woman on the crew."

The Muslim woman didn't seem to understand what Meg meant, so she continued.

"You can use it first, and by yourself. The rest of us will take turns in the common shower until you're done. I know it's not perfect, but will that work?"

The woman nodded and almost broke a smile across her mouth. She wiped at her tears and held her baby to her. The infant stirred and let out a meek cry.

"She is hungry," the woman said, and a new look of discomfort fell across her face.

"You can use the engineer's room for that, too. It has a door that locks."

Rex had come to stand near Meg. He seemed unhappy they were paying so much attention to the Muslim woman, but he didn't say anything. The other survivors were all too shocked to do anything but stand there huddled together, so Meg turned to go up the stairs, motioning for them to follow.

"Eric and me will keep an eye out," Rex said, his voice echoing up behind Meg as she climbed the stairs.

The shower turned out better than Meg thought it would. The soap stung, and the sponge she used to wash herself was about as soft as a handful of dry sand. But it's what they had available, and at the end of it she was clean and felt safe from any contamination.

She'd broken out a supply of sponges and given one to each of the survivors. Mothers had to share with their children so they'd have enough, and that mostly went over okay. Only one person grumbled about *the Muslim girl* getting her own sponge, and one for her baby, and a shower all to herself. Meg wanted to say something, but knew better. Tension was high enough already, and xenophobia would become a problem no matter what Meg had to say. She could either come down hard on these people or let them learn the lesson on their own.

Better that we all learn to swallow our pride in our own way. We'll survive by sticking together.

With each of them showered, and Meg in her full turnout gear again, they gathered on the app floor to settle in and talk about their plans for the coming night.

— 14 —

Sunnyside, Queens

The corporal next to Jed scanned the rooftops as they moved down Queens Boulevard. They'd just crossed the intersection with Grand Avenue and Broadway when Jed caught movement in an empty lot at the corner. A flash of something small and white near the fence surrounding the lot. Construction cranes sat there, empty and dead, but in weird positions, like they'd been left in a rush. A Bobcat was jammed up next to the fence. Its little loader bucket was raised all the way, like somebody had used it to jump out of the lot.

That's where Jed thought he'd seen movement, right by the Bobcat. Another flash of white caught his eye. But then they were past the lot and moving deeper into Elmhurst.

Just a cat, or a raccoon or some shit.

The convoy rolled on, but would slow sometimes at intersections, and a metal screeching would echo down the street. The first time it happened, Jed couldn't figure it out until his truck moved through the intersection. The wrecked cars that had blocked the road sat in heaps, tangled up and smashed together. The lead truck had pushed them out of the way. It wasn't like that at every corner, but it happened often enough that Jed worried they'd get ambushed by the monsters. But the city was really quiet. Like, he'd never seen New York so quiet, not even on a Sunday morning when everyone was supposed to be in church. Still had the bums and crackheads staggering around the 'hood at least.

But now, it was like the city was dead already. Nothing but a stray cat darting under a bush to hide, and wrecked cars here and there. He glimpsed another flash of white up high on an apartment and Jed felt his finger curl around the trigger. He lifted his muzzle and scanned the buildings nearby. A boy peeked from behind a curtain in a second story apartment window. The kid waved at Jed.

Little dude probably thinks we're all here to save him. Shit.

Jed would've saved the kid if he had to, but that would mean stopping the truck and walking around on the street, climbing over wrecked cars and trash. And bodies. Jed had wondered if the monsters took people away to eat. He hadn't seen any bodies when he and Chips were running that morning, or when he'd hooked up with the Army guys outside his grandma's place. But he saw the bodies now. Lots of them, all tangled up inside the cars, bloody and broken apart. And the street up ahead was filled with corpses.

The kid was probably still back there waving as the last truck in the convoy rolled past his apartment. Jed felt a tug on his heart for a second, but he knew there was no saving that kid. There was no saving anybody but himself.

The soldiers behind him must have seen the kid, because they started talking up a storm. Jed was going to tell them he'd seen the kid and wished they could have helped him, but one of the other guys started firing. The sergeant up front hollered "Cease fire! Cease fire!" and gave the hand sign as he rushed back and slapped the soldier's hand away from his trigger.

"The fuck's the matter with you, son? You hear the order to light it up? Who gave the order? Corporal Haskins," the sergeant yelled at the black dude next to Jed.

"Yes, Sergeant," the corporal said back.

"Keep your squad in line!" The sergeant gave the soldier who'd started shooting another whack on the helmet.

The soldier shrank back, but didn't say anything. The sergeant gave the whole truck a glare and went back to his position up front.

"Eyes out, on the city. High and low. And you *report* when you see something. You do *not* fire until you are ordered to do so. Hooah?"

Every man in the truck replied, and Jed joined in, even though he was watching the truck behind them. They were second to last in the convoy, and the one in the back was lagging a bit.

"Sergeant," Jed said.

"What?" the man said, not turning around.

"The truck in back. They're—"

"You supposed to be watching the truck behind us or your zone of fire, Private?"

"My—Shit!"

As Jed and now the other soldiers watched, the rear truck jerked, skidded sideways and began to tip. The men in the back held on, trying to stay in the bed, but the truck went up on one set of wheels and came crashing down on its side. Soldiers spilled out of the bed and landed on the pavement.

Up front in Jed's truck, the sergeant banged on the cab and yelled for them to stop.

"First squad, dismount! Second squad, cover them and watch for movement. You see anything looks hostile, *now* you shoot it."

Jed wasn't sure, but he thought something sprayed inside the cab of the last truck in the split second before it went over. He was going to say something, but he felt the man behind him pushing him. Then the sergeant gave him an earful.

"Let's go, Welch!" the sergeant yelled.

Corporal Haskins was already off the truck and moving with his weapon up, getting closer to the soldiers lying in the street. One of them wasn't moving at all, but the others were all rolling around holding their arms or sides, except for one guy who was up on his feet and backpedaling from the truck.

"Hey," Haskins called out to the guy. "You wanna help them up? Some of them hurt."

Jed jumped off the truck and moved to join the guy who was backing away. He looked like he knew what was up and didn't want any part of it.

Only fool out here has any sense. Shit's going down. We should just go. Get the guys ain't hurt and just go.

Jed caught up to the guy and put a hand on his shoulder. The soldier spun around and had his rifle up in Jed's grill.

"Stay the fuck off me!" the soldier screamed at him. The guy was just a kid, barely out of high school probably. And his face was crazy, like he'd seen the inside of hell.

Jed backed off and the dude lowered his rifle. But he kept stepping backwards, moving his head left to right and looking like you did when the big kids find you on the schoolyard in summer. His eyes were all big and his mouth kept shaking like he wanted to say something. Jed got a few more steps away from the kid and went back to scanning the area. Corporal Haskins held a position between the trucks. He was right out in the open, watching the street and the high rises across the way. The rest of the squad from Jed's truck had reached the guys who fell and were helping them up.

The sergeant shouted something. Then Jed heard the *pop-pop-pop* of M16s. He scanned around the trucks and spotted movement again, from one of the high rise apartments across the boulevard.

But the gunfire was aimed down low, street level somewhere, and Jed couldn't see anything to shoot at from where he was. Corporal Haskins fired at something across the street while the rest of the squad helped the injured guys get to the truck. Jed tucked back up against tailgate. He was in full view of the injured guys and the squad helping them, so he did his best to act like he was holding a covering position. Jed scanned the area with his weapon at the ready and kept flashing a glance at the corporal, who was popping off rounds.

Jed almost saw the monsters in time. He'd turned to check where the crazy kid had gone. He heard something back there, at the edge of the street, and was looking around the end of the truck to see what it was. Then a swarm of the monsters just tore into Haskins. The

99

corporal vanished under a knot of sickly white skin and sprays of blood. Jed pivoted and brought his weapon up in time to take out one that was coming his way, charging at him on all fours like a mad dog. He lit it up with three rounds to the chest, and the monster fell on its face with blood leaking out of everything.

Haskins was done, just gone under the mass of shrieking monsters that leaped on him. A foot and one hand were all Jed could see of the man. Jed heard more gunfire from the truck now, and the sergeant was still shouting. The guys in the street scrambled for the truck, and two of them had to stop to reposition the unconscious guy they were carrying.

Jed went to help and reached a hand to take the injured guy's weapon, but they all barged into Jed and shoved him out of their way.

"Just fucking shoot them!" one of the soldiers yelled at him as they moved for the truck bed. "Shoot the fucking things!"

Jed backed up a step. He lifted his weapon, but the half dozen monsters that had taken out Haskins were all dead now, shot to shit by the guys still in the truck. A series of shrieks and growls echoed across the boulevard and Jed looked in the direction of the sound, across the street. A cascade of pale white flesh raced down the high rises, like ants pouring out of a hive. He could hear their joints clicking and snapping as they moved, and the shrieks and snarls they made nearly turned Jed's stomach inside out. He backed up another step, bumping into the truck. Someone up there was yelling his name, telling him to get up on the truck. But Jed knew where he was going. He turned on his heels and ran like hell.

***

Shouts and gunfire shifted to screams and howls of pain behind him. Jed raced down a street that cut off the boulevard and ran between two buildings, sucking in air and pushing it out as fast as he could. He skidded to a stop when he heard a car alarm nearby. Lights flashed in time with the alarm on a BMW with tinted windows. The car was angled into a parking space behind the buildings. The driver's side door was open, but Jed didn't see any movement. He brought his weapon up and went closer until he saw blood on the ground, and then an M16 lying beside the rear bumper.

Jed went closer still, keeping some distance from the car as he went around the bumper. The crazy kid from before had been torn up and left in a heap on the other side of the car. Blood spattered across the doors on the passenger side, and the windshield was smashed in like something big had landed on it.

Jed snapped his rifle up and aimed at the roof of the building beside him. It was two stories high, just like the row houses across the way. Jed scanned left and right and moved to the kid's body. He still had ammo on him.

Right as Jed reached for the kid's LBE harness, the body twitched and the legs began kicking. The kid was still alive. His chest was ripped up and blood was all over him, but he was still alive.

Jed didn't waste a second before he aimed and fired right into his chin. A bloody mess spattered from inside the kid's helmet and his body went still again. Waiting a beat, Jed kept his aim but flicked his head back and forth, and up, to check for movement.

He looked at the kid's ammo pouches now. They were dripping with blood. He'd have to touch it. In a rush, Jed backed away from the kid's body, casting around the area as he moved out, making sure nothing had snuck up to watch him. He'd seen the way the swarm moved from the high rises. He'd also seen one of them sitting on top of a parked car, watching the others.

Fucking things ain't zombies, like that dude said. They can think. They're smart as hell.

Jed could still hear the *pop-pop* of small arms from back where the trucks were. An engine roared and then cut out and Jed heard the screeching of metal on metal. He moved across the street, farther from the sounds and the screams.

The row houses behind him were all painted dark colors, some of them red and others brown or black. Trees shaded the fronts and concealed the windows, but Jed could tell some of the houses were occupied, and not by monsters. Curtains flicked back and forth and faces peered out from some windows.

A scream from down the street put Jed on the move in the other direction. He ran, ducking low behind parked cars and keeping an eye on rooftops and trees as he went. He had to get inside. If he stayed out on the street—

Shrieking and howling echoed into the afternoon sky along with more gunfire. Something big opened up a few streets over and Jed felt the heavy *choop-choop* of a grenade launcher, followed by a string of detonations that shook some of the houses nearby. He was careful to keep an eye out this time, watching for movement anywhere in his area. With his rifle up, Jed scanned left to right, from the street level up to the rooftops.

Left to right. Up and down. Left to—

Two of them came crawling like spiders down the walls of a house on his side of the street.

They had shreds of clothing still on, and Jed could see they were both women before they changed. Jed lifted his rifle and aimed at one of them. Another string of explosions rocked the city around him. The thing on the wall snapped its head up and stared straight at Jed. He fired, putting a round right into its mouth.

It dropped like a dead cockroach, straight down to the sidewalk.

Its partner reared back and shrieked long and high. Jed pulled his shoulders up tight, trying to block his ears. Then the monster jumped for a tree next to the house. It climbed down branch to branch, moving like it was out for Jed's blood. He shifted his aim and fired, but it was too fast and his shots missed. The monster made it to the lowest branch and seemed to hold there, like it had forgotten why it was climbing down instead of up.

The monster clawed at its own chest, leaving deep gouges in its pasty white flesh. Thick lines of blood drooled down its skin and it shrieked again. Jed went into flight mode. He turned and ran, slowing every few steps to spin back and fire off a three-round burst.

At the end of the block, Jed heard shouting and more gunfire from a few streets up. The one behind him jumped from parked cars and up into trees, onto the walls of houses and down to the street. It stopped to claw at itself sometimes, or to bite its arm before leaping after him again. Jed fired a burst at it and missed. At this rate, he'd have to change magazines before he hit it.

"Stay still, motherfucker," Jed shouted as he paused against a van parked on the street. He fired another burst. He only had three rounds left in the magazine before he had to change. The monster was getting closer, leaping from car to tree, to the wall of the nearest house. It hung there, staring at him before jumping to the sidewalk and scrambling on all fours straight at him. It slid left and right as it moved, like it knew he had to aim to hit it.

"Shit! Stay fucking still!" Jed screamed, as he held his rifle with shaking hands and squeezed the last three round burst out of the magazine.

— 15 —

Upper East Side, Manhattan

"It seems like it's over," Rex said while Meg made sure the survivors all had blankets on their cots. They bundled up extra uniforms for pillows, and even pulled the couch cushions from the day room.

"I don't know about it being over," Meg said when they were done with the cots. "But it does seem quieter. If any of them try to get inside, we have the hose," Meg said, motioning at Eric. He was still by the door to the chief's office with the hose wrapped around him and the nozzle up and ready.

The survivors sat on their cots, looking shifty and uncertain. The Muslim woman, who was named Abeer, held her baby close and sat off to the side of the main group. She'd been given a few looks and stares from some of the survivors. Still others seemed ready to just ignore her. Meg realized she couldn't let it continue this way, so she said what had been on her mind the minute the survivors showed up.

"Look everyone, we might be all that's left. We don't have radio contact with anyone out there."

"What?" Rex asked, surprised.

"I checked while I was upstairs," Meg said. "The phone's dead. So whatever information we have is contained right here." Meg tapped a finger against her temple. "And whatever chance of survival we have left, it's right here," she said, tapping her finger over her heart.

The group stared at her, even Eric, but he had a smile on his face. "Tell 'em, Meg," he said.

"For now, *we* are all any of us have. That means that you, me, the person next to you, any one of us might be the one who saves your life. So we'd better get used to knowing each other and treating each other like family."

As Meg finished, a few sirens sounded from distant neighborhoods, and gunfire popped off nearby. The survivors, as one, looked to the shutter doors. One of them held her hands up to her throat in fear. She was a heavyset white woman in a thick pink sweater and plaid skirt, like the kind Meg had seen in too many office dramas back when she watched television.

Before I met Tim and took up running as a hobby instead of holding down couches.

The large woman said, "We don't have any guns. What if those are criminals out there? We aren't armed!"

"Yes we are," Meg said. "And I don't think those are criminals. The only people I saw with weapons were the Army, and a couple of guys trying to kill those things. I'm sure there are bad seeds out there, but for now I'd say we're safe. Criminals will probably go for banks and liquor stores, and not necessarily in that order."

That comment got Meg a few laughs, but the pink sweater woman wasn't impressed.

"I don't see any guns here."

"That's because this is a fire house, ma'am. We don't have guns. We have axes," Meg said, holding hers up and using it to point out others that hung in a rack along the wall.

"What about food?" a dark-skinned woman asked. She sat in the front of the group with her young daughter by her side. The girl had pigtails and a look on her face to match her mother's. But she held a hand over her stomach like she hadn't eaten in a while. The girl couldn't have been older than six or seven.

"We have two pantries full of dry goods. Plenty of crackers, cookies, and pasta. Cans and jars. Plus the shift fridge. If we eat through that, we'll dip into the other fridge."

"How can we cook it?" the pink sweater lady asked. "I mean some food you can heat up in a microwave, but…"

"We have a kitchen, ma'am. Upstairs in the day room. Full stove, oven, and yes, a microwave. We won't starve, at least as long as the power holds out. After that, I suppose we can start a fire somehow."

That got more laughs, and from almost everybody. Meg let the glimmer of happiness swell into a smile, even for just a second.

Might be the last time we laugh for a long while.

"The food isn't a buffet, but it'll keep us from going hungry tonight."

"We'll need medicine," an older black woman said. She was the one from the door, with the gloves on her hands. She'd taken them off upstairs before she showered. Now she sat beside the mother and her daughter, and she still had the same determined look on her face. "I need to take my dailies. If I don't—Well, it's a wonder my heart is still ticking, but you know what I'm saying."

Meg nodded. "I do, ma'am, and I'm sorry we don't have more to offer. There's a pharmacy a few blocks over. If it ends up looking safe, we can probably get what you need there. Later."

Meg paused, looking at the group of survivors. "Like I said, we really don't know anything more than you all do. If the military can be trusted—"

A loud laugh stopped Meg and she looked to the person who had complained about Abeer getting her own shower. The young woman sat on the opposite side of the group, but also at the edge, like she was announcing how much of an outcast she was.

"Did you have something to say, ma'am?"

"Do I have—What is this, fucking Kindergarten?" the girl shot back. When she showed her whole face, Meg could see the girl was probably a teenager, maybe in her early twenties at most. She had a shock of blue hair stuck to one side of her head that mostly hung down in front of her eye. The rest of her head was shaved and she had more jewelry in her face than Meg had ever owned in her life.

"No," Meg said, keeping her cool as best she could. "This isn't Kindergarten. It's either the end of the world or, at best, an epidemic like nothing we've ever seen. Whichever is true, I don't really care. My only goal is to keep us all alive and safe. As I was say—"

"Yeah, as you were saying," the punk girl interrupted. "If the military can be trusted. Like, you know they're probably the ones that did this, right? It's, like, the fucking military is always experimenting and shit. Making up zombie plagues to go and fuck up the other guys, except now they've fucked us in—"

"Miss," Meg finally said, with a hand up for the girl to stop. "You need to watch your language. There are young people in the room. Some even younger than *you*. As for the disease, we don't know exactly where this came from or why. But we do know how. It's not Ebola, but it is a similar virus. That's what the soldiers I've spoken to told me. It is spread by a blood borne pathogen. So from now on, we stay away from the chief's office and nobody touches anything that's got blood on it. When help comes, we'll signal them with the station alarm and open the shutters to let them in."

"What if it isn't help?" the punk girl asked. She was still clearly on edge, but she'd softened a bit from her earlier outburst.

"If it isn't help, we have the hose. Eric, Rex, and I will keep watch during the night. The rest of you should split up, take the extra turnout jackets for protection and warmth. Some of you can go upstairs to the dorm room or the day room and get some sleep. The rest will have to stay down here. I'm sorry we don't have more space."

Meg could tell an argument was about to start about who should get the upstairs, and whether Rex or Eric would get the captain's office while Meg took the engineer's bed. Abeer sat up straight, but her face told Meg she was worried for her safety. Meg cleared her throat and added to her last statement.

"Unless you feel like you can fight, you should go upstairs. If you do think you can fight, we'll get you a full turnout suit and an axe."

"Um, Meg," Rex said, coming back from where he'd

been standing by the shutter doors. "It looks like somebody's out there now. I don't think it's—I mean, it's more survivors. I think."

"He thinks," the punk girl said. "Or he knows? We're not letting anyone in here."

"We're doing what it takes to stay alive and to help anyone we can," Meg said, silencing the blue haired girl with a look.

"Show me, Rex."

Meg followed the man's heavy tread as he went down the floor to the shutters. He stood on tip toe and peered out, coming back down with a nod of his head.

"Yep. Looks like two of ours. They're at the engine."

Meg went up on the shutter and looked outside. The sky was overcast and the skyscrapers threw deeper shadows onto the street in front of the house. But Meg could pick out the two firefighters over by the crashed engine. They wore full turnout gear and were digging through materials that had spilled from the truck when it slammed into the parked car. One of them came up with a Nomex mask and quickly strapped it on.

"They're okay," Meg said. "We have to get them inside. Now!"

— 16 —

Jed's shots went into the sidewalk, missing the monster completely. It skittered to its right and leaped up on the wall of the house. Jed put his back against the van and held his weapon up. Even thought it was empty, it was the only thing between him and death.

The monster stared at Jed with those narrow yellow cat eyes. It hissed at him through its ugly ass sucker mouth and tensed like it would jump for the van behind him. Jed almost took a hand off his weapon to reach for his ammo pouch. But the creature kept flicking its tongue around its puffy lips as it watched him. He couldn't risk changing magazines now. He could try for the Glock on his hip, but he knew if he moved his hands off the rifle, it would jump. It kept flicking its glare back and forth from Jed's muzzle to the top of the van.

It knows the weapon is a threat. It knows what a gun can do.

Fine, so the monsters were smart. They knew a threat when they saw one. Jed had to hope they didn't know how to count bullets, otherwise he was done. He kept his aim on the ugly beast's face and waited for it to move. It

111

did, but not in the direction he thought it would.

Jed lifted his aim, thinking the monster was going to jump for the van and get behind him. But it just lifted up and leaped forward, landing on the sidewalk right in front of Jed.

"Shit!" Jed screamed.

He backed up tighter against the van and slid along its length, trying to get some distance before the monster jumped at him again. It just sat there, though, staring at him, like it was toying with him.

Jed had to risk reloading. He reached a shaking hand to his ammo pouch and unclipped it. The monster still sat on the sidewalk staring at him.

Okay, so they don't know what makes the gun go bang. That's good.

Jed had the pouch open and was slipping a magazine out when he heard the clicking sound behind him. He spun around just as another one swiped at his head from on top of the van.

A clawed hand went by Jed's face so close he could smell the stink of rotting fruit coming off its skin. He lifted his rifle up to block the next hand that came for him. He felt the thing strike out at his weapon and grab hold of it. Then he heard the clicking and popping of joints from the one on the sidewalk behind him. It was closing in fast. Jed almost twisted his own neck trying to get a look at it, but he had to keep an eye on the one on the van. It had his weapon held tight.

Jed pulled back on the M16, then felt the rifle yanked out of his grip, leaving him empty-handed. He tumbled against the van, nearly fell over his own feet, but just got away from the grabbing hands behind him. He snapped a hand at the holster on his hip and tugged on the Glock. He had it halfway out, but fumbled it when something caught his LBE and yanked. He was hauled backwards and thrown up against the van so hard he lost his breath. The Glock clattered to the sidewalk and under the van.

Jed put a hand out and closed his eyes, knowing it was hopeless. He was fucked.

"Get down!" someone shouted from just down the street. Gunfire popped out and Jed heard bullets zipping by him. He waited, opening his eyes and staring at the one in front of him, hoping it would go down. But the rounds all missed. The monster looked like it was dancing as it roved back and forth across the sidewalk, flicking its head in the direction of the shooter and then looking back at Jed.

More gunfire came, and still missed, but chips of concrete flecked up against the van and peppered Jed's legs. The monsters split up. Jed heard the one on the van jump away, throwing Jed's rifle into the street as it did. The plastic clatter made his heart sink. He could go for the Glock, but it was under the van, and the one on the sidewalk stayed close, stalking him from just a foot away, like a cat around a mouse. He didn't dare drop to all fours and try to fish the gun out of the gutter.

Jed felt the warm trickle of piss down his leg, and the monster seemed to sense it. It stopped and lifted its nose, sniffing at the air and coming closer. Jed could smell its funky skin, like moldy fruit all warm and thick. It shrieked at him, spattering his boots with saliva.

Then its head vanished in a spray of blood and bone as the *pa-pa-pop* of a three-round burst echoed in Jed's ears.

He stayed up against the van, half-crying and half ready to just fall to his knees and give the fuck up.

I didn't sign up for this. Didn't sign up for none of this.

He wasn't even in the Marines anymore; and if he was, he sure as hell wouldn't be trying to take the fight to monsters.

Fucking nuke 'em, just burn 'em out.

"Gotta just burn 'em out," he said through his sobs and tears.

"What's your name?" someone asked from a few feet away. "You hit? Did it get you?"

Jed kept mumbling about burning the things up, talking into his shirt. But whoever was yelling at him clearly didn't want to wait around.

"Hey, answer me or I'ma light you up to be safe."

"No!" Jed shouted, toppling backwards as he moved from where he'd squatted down by the van. He slid along it again and ended up on his ass next to the body of the thing that was about to eat his face off. A Marine with a weapon raised was coming toward him from a little ways down the sidewalk. Jed could see the body of the other monster behind the man.

"Stay back from the body!" the Marine yelled at Jed. "Do not make contact with the infected."

Jed stopped moving and looked behind him. He'd nearly put his hand in the puddle of blood leaking out of the thing's half gone head. He looked around the street and up at the rooftops. He didn't see any of the monsters, and the gunfire and shrieking seemed to be tapering off nearby. Jed looked back at the Marine in front of him. He was a white guy, a little younger than Jed, and he had an M16 aimed at Jed's chest. The dude's rank wasn't visible, so Jed just went with what felt right.

"I'm Welch. Private Welch. Was with the—" he tried to remember the unit he'd been assigned to by the First Sergeant back on the ball fields.

"You Army?" the Marine asked.

"Marines. I was—I'm out. Since Iraq. But the—Civil Affairs guys," he said, remembering the unit name finally. "They set me up with some gear. Told me I could keep my Glock." Jed made to reach under the van, but the Marine looked like he was ready to shoot him. Jed kept his hand away from the gun.

"What're you doing here?" the Marine asked him. "Where's your unit?"

"On the boulevard. They—We gotta go, man. There's a ton of them things. Comin' outta the apartments." Jed jerked his head in the direction of Queens Boulevard.

The Marine lowered his rifle and offered a hand to help Jed up.

"You seem all right. My name's Rainey. Go'on get your weapon. We'll get back to my platoon."

Jed looked at Rainey as the Marine stared off down the street. He seemed like he was keeping watch, but something in his face told Jed he had more on his mind.

"Your platoon's around here?" Jed asked.

"Yeah. What's left of 'em," Rainey said. "Let's go, Welch. It's quiet now. Won't stay that way for long."

Jed got up; he tried to cover the stain of piss on his crotch. Rainey didn't notice, or didn't say anything if he did. He turned and started away from the area, heading out at a trot. Jed went to grab the Glock, but he stopped short. Blood from the dead monster's head drained down into the gutter off the edge of the sidewalk, covering the gun.

Fuck, fuck, fuck.

Jed got to his feet and jogged around the van. He snapped up his rifle from where it had landed after the monster threw it in the street. It was banged up a little; one corner of the ejector cover was bent and the stock had a crack in it. Jed slapped a fresh magazine in and charged the weapon. It seemed to work fine, but Jed kept throwing nervous glances at the rifle as he ran to catch up to Rainey.

"Hey, I heard the Corps was clearing the city, mopping up the monsters."

"Who told you that?" Rainey asked. He kept scanning their route, with his rifle up and ready. Jed followed suit before he replied.

"Some dickhead NCO back at the fields. That's where the Civil Affairs guys were set up. My old school, man."

Rainey didn't reply. Jed was happy to have someone with him, but Rainey seemed like he'd rather keep quiet than talk about shit. Jed just kept his eyes on the street and rooftops as they moved.

They rounded corners and went down streets, all the while watching the rooftops and alleys between houses for any sign of the monsters. They went under Roosevelt Avenue and came into a neighborhood with more high rises and apartments. Jed noticed fewer and fewer curtains being moved aside, and more and more front doors and ground-floor windows smashed in.

And more blood and bodies lying on front walks and near cars still parked on the street, like people got taken out right as they were about to get away.

"They're getting inside," he said. "Getting everybody, man."

"Yep," was Rainey's short reply. He kept his weapon shouldered and scanned as they moved. Left to right, up and down.

After a few blocks of stalking like that, Rainey put a hand up to hold position. Jed drew up against the nearest wall. They were next to a library on a corner, with a little park across the street in one direction, and a public school across the other street. Jed looked into the trees, thinking they should be over there instead of out on the damn street. They didn't have any cover here, and Jed felt like a sitting goddamned duck in the open.

He started to say they should get hid somewhere, but Rainey swatted a hand backwards in the air while he scanned the street ahead.

Jed still didn't know Rainey's rank. The guy acted like he knew his shit, and Jed didn't really mind taking orders from him either. It was just weird not knowing if the guy telling you to shut your hole was an NCO or a private.

"My platoon should be up ahead, Welch. Rally point was the park on the other side of that school. See it?"

Jed grunted to say he did. He knew the school. They were across from PS11.

Memo got jumped by some kids when he went here.

It was quiet and dark around the schoolyard. The closer Jed looked, the more he recognized the same signs of entry and damage as he had in the other buildings around them. He looked at the high rise building to the left of the school, and his breath caught in his throat.

"The—They ain't still there," he said, pointing at high rise. The windows were all smashed out on the upper floors, and streaks of what had to be blood dripped down the side of the building from where people had either jumped through the glass or been thrown through it.

Rainey shook his head, and Jed didn't miss his voice cracking a bit when he said, "Damn. Oh damn."

"Hey," someone shouted from the cluster of trees to their right. Jed and Rainey looked together, bringing their weapons up.

"Hold your fire," the unseen speaker said. A second later a Marine came out from the trees with his own weapon up and at the ready. Rainey lowered his weapon a bit, but kept both hands on it. Jed did the same and waited for the other Marine to identify himself. Rainey handled the introductions for him.

"That you, Sergeant Townsend?"

"Yeah. Now c'mon get over here."

Rainey moved out, giving Jed a half glance and nodding his head for him to follow. They crossed the street quickly and got under the trees with the NCO.

Sergeant Townsend was about Jed's height, just under six feet. He was black and the look in his eyes told Jed he was a man you trusted. Something in how he held his head up and looked right at you. He didn't seem to judge Jed for anything, and for a moment Jed forgot that he'd been trying to get away from the military and forget all about ever being a Marine.

"Who're you, son?" Sergeant Townsend asked.

"Private Welch, Sergeant. I was with the Civil Affairs guys, but I used to be in the Corps. Got out and—"

"All right," Sergeant Townsend said, putting up a hand. "All right. Don't need your life story right now.

118

'Used to be' is as good as *you are*, am I right, Marine?"

Jed paused only a second before nodding and saying "Rah."

The NCO chuckled, but it was a laugh like you'd give a homie. Jed couldn't keep the smile off his face, so he turned his head left and right, looking at where they'd ended up and what was around them now.

"Where's the rest of 'em, Sergeant?" Rainey asked.

"Platoon got tore up. Me and Sergeant Baxter's squad is all that's left. They already moved out. I stayed back in case any of y'all came through."

"Shit," Rainey said. "Kehoe and Campbell gone?"

Sergeant Townsend just nodded. Rainey said something under his breath, and Jed heard that little catch in his voice again, like he was about ready to curl up and start crying for his baby bottle.

"C'mon now," Sergeant Townsend said. "They gone so we can stay alive to remember 'em. And I'm all outta straws, Marine."

Rainey recovered a bit at that. Jed stayed quiet for a beat before he asked, "What's the plan, Sergeant? Seems quiet now."

And it was. The shrieking, if they heard any at all, was really far off, and they hadn't heard any gunfire since before Roosevelt Avenue.

"Shit's too quiet," Sergeant Townsend said. "Got no radio contact, so we're looking at a hump down to the East River and over Queensbridge. Should be a checkpoint this end. Headquarters Company set it up before they sent us out into this motherfucker. You seen combat, Welch?" he asked at the end, looking more closely at Jed's uniform and weapon.

"Yeah—Yes, Sergeant. I was in Iraq."

Sergeant Townsend didn't seem to question Jed's words. Or, if he did, he didn't make any noise about it.

"C'mon," the NCO said, leaving the cover of the trees and scanning the street in front of PS11. Jed and Rainey followed him out.

"We gotta move," Sergeant Townsend said, stepping off down the sidewalk. "Checkpoint's closing down at sunset."

"What's happening then?" Jed asked. He and Rainey had to jog to keep up with the NCO.

Sergeant Townsend picked up the pace a bit, and answered between breaths. "They pulling back to Manhattan," he said. "And blowing the bridges."

— 17 —

Upper East Side, Manhattan

With the two new firefighters, a man and a woman, safely inside, Rex helped Meg ratchet the shutters closed. Every creak and groan of the metal door was like an explosion in Meg's ears. The firefighters they'd just welcomed told them to close the door as quietly as possible.

"They're attracted to noise. Or sounds of any kind really," the woman had said the instant she was inside. Her partner took the mask off while she introduced them. Her name was Rachel Beal. She was a few inches over Meg's 5' 8" frame and from her high, broad shoulders, Meg figured the woman was an athlete. Her dark skin and feline features made Meg think of her cat, Biggins.

She let the memory go and shook Rachel's hand.

Rachel's partner was almost a carbon copy of Rex, except his name was Jason Weekes and his hair was blond instead of red.

"Jason, Rachel," Meg said. "Welcome to our little corner of hell."

They both nodded their thanks before Jason filled everyone in on the situation outside.

"The Army and Marines are pulling back to Manhattan Island. They're supposed to blow the bridges—"

"*What?*" Rex shouted. "They can't *do* that. My folks are down in Brooklyn."

"If your families… If *any* of your families are in the city, they're probably safe. The military's been really good about evacuating affected areas."

Meg wondered if Jason's definition of *really good* matched hers. How many husbands and neighbors did the military think it was okay to lose before they downgraded *really good* to *not so hot*? Or *just plain shitty*?

"You've seen this?" Meg asked, feeling the burn of anger and frustration finally boiling over. "The evacuations, I mean. Because I have. I was evacuated from my home. They had to kill my husband first, though. He'd become a monster and killed a cop, and our neighbor and his wife. He would have killed me next if they hadn't shot him."

Neither Jason nor Rachel had anything to say. They, and everyone else, just stared back at Meg as she felt the hot tears flowing down her cheeks. Finally, Abeer stepped forward from the group.

"I am sorry for your husband," Abeer said. "My husband's name was Abdallah. The soldiers had to shoot him. I miss him."

Meg nodded and wiped her tears. "Thank you, Abeer."

"I don't mean to ignore anyone's suffering," Rachel said. "But we have to secure this place. The front door is wide open, and those lockers aren't going to hold them for more than a minute at best. I've seen them fight and move. They can climb—"

"*I know!*" Meg shouted and then put a hand over her

mouth, remembering the monsters were attracted to sounds. She pulled in a sob, dropped her hand, and bowed her head. "I know. I'm sorry."

Distant gunfire echoed through the city outside. It sounded like a popcorn maker out of control at first, but Meg quickly realized what it was.

"That's the Army," one of the survivors said. "It has to be. They'll save us."

"Don't count on it," Jason said. "They're doing well, like I said. A lot of the city is already evac'd to Manhattan, and they have checkpoints at the bridges."

"So what's the problem?" Rex asked.

Jason stared at him for a beat before replying. "I've seen them go right through a whole platoon of armed soldiers. I'm talking machine guns, rocket launchers. And still the monsters won. It isn't pretty."

That seemed to shake everyone up, and the room fell silent. Meg looked to Eric, who stayed at his post facing the door to the chief's office with the hose around his waist.

"Eric, how many masks do we have?"

Before Eric could reply, Rex answered her. "About a dozen, counting the one they brought in."

"We should keep at least one down here for whoever is on guard. The rest, put them on the children first. Then the parents. After that go by age, starting with the youngest."

Rex looked ready to protest Meg's order, but the other firefighters in the room all nodded their approval. Rex stood on shaky legs and waved for the survivors to follow him to the back of the bay. The older black woman led the way staying right behind Rex. She was followed by

Abeer and her baby, then the mother and her daughter in pigtails right behind her. The others trailed behind in a staggering line.

Meg kept her voice low and asked Jason and Rachel, "Is it really that bad out there? What's really going on? You haven't told us the whole story."

Jason shook his head. "No, we haven't. We don't really know. I said that about the military doing well because I could see those people needed some good news. But the truth is—"

"We're fucked," Rachel said, barely keeping her voice down. Some of the survivors looked their way and Meg let her face tell Rachel to cool it. The other woman seemed to get it. Rachel moved closer to the shutters and motioned for Meg and Jason to join her in looking out the windows. When they were all gathered at the far end of the floor, away from the survivors, Rachel continued, keeping her voice down this time.

"There is no coming back from this. Whatever it is, there is no cure, no treatment. Nothing. If you get attacked, you're dead. And if you're not dead, it doesn't matter because you're not human anymore either."

Rachel's words rattled Meg, and hard. She had to suck in a breath at the thought of what they were facing. The empty New York City street outside didn't help her mood, either. The street should have been filled with bumper to bumper traffic, and people all over the sidewalks.

Meg should be looking for bicycle messengers whipping down the street between cars, and holding her breath every time a taxi or truck or van merged without checking for the cyclist. She'd seen it happen so many times, and almost every time the messenger pulled a fast dodge to avoid being crushed or run down. But Meg couldn't forget the times when it hadn't gone as well and she'd had to rush into the street to try and save a young person's life.

"Look," Rachel said, cutting in on Meg's thoughts. "They're still pretty thin around here. The outbreak started by JFK and moved through Queens and Brooklyn like a hurricane. The Army and Marines have mostly held them from spreading across the river."

"But we've already seen them here," Meg said.

"I know. I said 'mostly'. But even if they clean out the ones that are here, they won't be able to guarantee anything come nightfall. There's a hardware store just up the street. It's been looted already, but there's plenty of lumber in the yard beside the store. I'm sure they have at least one hammer left and some nails. We need to barricade this place, and fast."

"Won't that make noise?" Eric asked. He must have come closer while Meg was busying herself with memories. She nodded at him and Eric let his attention settle on her and the others for a moment. Then he went back to watching the doorway.

"Everything makes noise," Rachel said. "But, yeah, you're right. We'll have to work fast, and the sooner we start, the better we'll be. I saw some of those monsters get caught in the sun when the clouds parted. They ran for the shadows. I think they're sensitive to sunlight. We don't have much of that left."

Meg looked at the house clock on the wall above an old Yankees team photo. The clock read nearly half past two.

"Eric," she said. "Can you hold the fort?"

"Don't worry," Jason said. "We'll get the wood. You guys make sure we can get back inside. But first, let's move that locker into the office to block the door."

Meg almost had to smile at him. As big as Rex, and with the same look in his eye that said he saw her as a woman first and firefighter second. But he had good ideas, and wasn't afraid of a little work.

With Rachel's help, they got the locker repositioned by lifting up each end and setting it down on a fire blanket. Then they pulled the blankets to shift the bulky metal case around without making as much noise as they had the first time Meg and Rex had moved it. When they had the front door mostly blocked with the locker, Jason and Rachel each put on a mask. Meg asked them to get more from the engine if it seemed clear.

"If you think it's safe to try," she said, already feeling guilty for sending them out on their own.

Meg and Eric opened the shutter door enough for Jason and Rachel to slip under it, then closed it again fast. Then they waited. Eric hoisted the hose again and paced between the doorway to the chief's office and the front of the floor by the shutters. Meg looked at Rex and the survivors at the back of the floor and thought about how many lives she had already failed to save that day.

— 18 —

Long Island City, Queens

Jed tried his best not to just fall the fuck out as they ran, but his breath came shorter and shorter.

"Sergeant Townsend," he said.

"Yeah."

The NCO was short on breath. They'd been running at a good pace down Skillman Avenue, passing empty row houses, storefronts, industrial buildings. Cars on the sidewalk sat there like nobody was coming back for them. An alarm beeped and whined from a block or so over. Somewhere a car door slammed shut and an engine turned over. But there was nobody around on the street. No shouting, no laughter. It was the only time in his life Jed had actually heard New York City without hearing the people in it.

"Yo, Welch. You got something?"

"Rail yards, Sergeant. Comin' up. Cross on...Honeywell."

"I know, Welch. Eyes out. Keep quiet."

Jed ignored the burn in his cheeks. He'd told Townsend about Honeywell because he knew the streets around here and figured he would help. Save them some time. They could cross on 39th or even at 43rd. Hell, they were about there now anyway. But those streets would take them up and away from the river.

Deeper into the neighborhoods. More places for them to hide. More places for me to die.

So far they'd only seen one of the things, and Rainey bagged it with a head shot from across the street. They'd had a clear run since then, but Jed could still hear gunfire not too far off, and mixed in with the sounds of big engines moving fast. If they could find a ride.

"We should boost the next car."

"You fuckin' crazy, Welch?" Rainey said.

Jed was about done taking shit and felt like it was time to dish a little back. Sergeant Townsend stopped him, though. "Y'all shut it down."

Jed nodded and went back to watching the rooftops as they ran. He wanted to give Rainey a look, but Sergeant Townsend was between them, and the tone of his voice just then told Jed not to fuck around even a little bit.

They ran on and Jed kept watch on the neighborhood. They passed some high rise apartments, and none of these had broken windows. A few storefronts did, and one or two of the row houses looked like they'd been raided. It wasn't too much farther to Honeywell, and then they'd just have to get out to the checkpoint at Queensbridge.

Ain't that far. I can do it. C'mon Jed, don't be a punk.

Right before 39th, in front of a big industrial building, Jed felt his side burn and then stab. Breathing got hard enough that he had to fall back a pace from the other two. He made it another block or so, but Jed was out of gas, and he knew it. His legs burned, the stitch in his side felt like a knife, and the damn LBE was rubbing like hell against his hips.

"Sergeant," he said. Then Jed was watching the street come up to meet his face. He got one hand out in time, and set the butt of his weapon on the street before his knees cracked down.

"The fuck?" Sergeant Townsend shouted. Jed struggled to one knee, ready to rise again. The NCO and Rainey slowed their pace and turned back to him.

"You comin', Welch?" the NCO asked.

They were still stepping backwards, and Rainey had his weapon up.

"I'm not bit, man," Jed said. "Just—Fuck, I can't keep up. I can't…"

He thought they would leave him there. They weren't coming back for him, and Rainey was about to turn and run. Jed could tell.

Sergeant Townsend brought his weapon up and scanned the area. They were at the edge of the rail yards now, just past 39th where Skillman jogged around the neighborhood. Some old burned up train cars sat on the tracks nearest them.

"Yo, Welch," Sergeant Townsend said, with that note in his voice that only an NCO could get.

They're gonna leave me behind.

"Sergeant, I—"

The roar of a truck motor put them all on alert. It was coming up a neighborhood street somewhere to their left. Rainey kept his weapon up, and Jed watched him trade a look with Sergeant Townsend. The NCO gave a nod and Rainey moved in a crouch; he followed Skillman to the mouth of the next street that went into the neighborhood. Sergeant Townsend kept watching the rooftops in between flashing a look at Jed.

He's waiting for me! Gotta do this. C'mon Jed. C'mon!

Jed got up on his feet, still shaky and still thinking the other guys were going to leave him behind. He got to his feet just as Rainey rushed back into the street with a grin on his face.

"It's them, Sergeant. The evac convoy."

"Hell yeah. Looks like you get that ride after all, Welch. C'mon, Marine. Keep up."

Jed coughed once, swallowed hard, and moved out after the other two Marines.

Might be back in the suck. But at least I'm alive.

***

The convoy was a line of three school buses led by a truck like the one Jed had been in before. He could make out the profile of a Hummer at the back. Looked like it had a heavy gun up top, but he couldn't be sure.

Inside the buses were crowds of scared civilians. They all had their faces up to the windows, looking everywhere except at each other. It was kids with their moms and dads mostly, but a few folks who looked like they were loners, or just old people who didn't have nobody else to come with them.

The truck up front had about a squad inside it. Weapons bristled out like spines, but they only had enough guys to cover the front and a little bit on both sides. Jed spotted a SAW up at the front. Everyone else up there had an M16.

Someone up there, probably another NCO, lifted a hand and waved at Sergeant Townsend. He double-timed it to the truck cab. The driver slowed down enough for him to hop on so he could talk to whoever was inside. After a few words went back and forth, the truck came to a stop and the buses and Hummer pulled up.

Everyone inside the buses started freaking out and Jed heard the screams of fear coming through the glass. Open palms slapped on he glass as the people hollered.

"Why are we stopped? Are they out there?"

"We have to go!"

Sergeant Townsend waved Rainey and Jed over and told them to get into the truck.

"Checkpoint's down. We're crossing with them. Mount up and take a zone of fire."

"Who are they?" Jed asked as they approached the truck.

"Army Civil Affairs. Sergeant Kuhn up front. You with them, Welch?"

Jed didn't rcmember anybody named Kuhn, but he double-checked to be sure. He didn't see any familiar faces. Jed hoped and prayed nobody in the truck had seen him take off back on the boulevard.

None of the other four guys gave him any notice, though. They were all too busy watching the neighborhood. Jed let out a sigh he didn't know he'd been holding. But when him and Rainey got up on the tailgate, Jed's heart sank.

Sergeant Boon was in the bed of the truck, lying on a stretcher with his hands bandaged up like they'd been torn to shit. He had a bloody stain running down both arms. Jed covered a zone of fire on the left side next to one of the CA guys. Rainey came up after Jed, putting him in the middle. Sergeant Townsend went to the rear of the truck. With the two CA guys on the other side, and the NCO and SAW gunner up front, they had a full perimeter now. The truck moved out and the buses followed.

Jed thought about Boon and hoped he hadn't spotted him. A second later his gut turned over and he thought he might spew over the side of the truck.

"That you, Hardcore Welch? The fuck you doing here?"

Jed risked a quick glance over his shoulder before going back to watching the neighborhood. "Sergeant Boon? You—They get you?" he asked over his shoulder.

"The fuck's it look like, *Hardcore*? I asked you why you're here."

The other guys couldn't help but hear their conversation, and Jed knew he had about two seconds to make it all go right or Boon would fuck him.

"I'm with them, Sergeant," he said, nodding in Rainey and Sergeant Townsend's direction.

"Your old unit," Sergeant Boon said, and he didn't make any effort to hide his doubt about Jed.

— 19 —

Upper East Side, Manhattan

Meg held the firehose ready while Eric and Rex helped haul two loaded flatbed carts into the app floor. Rachel and Jason had piled the carts with a stack of two by four lumber, some hammers and a box of nails, and a few sheets of thick plywood. Jason shook his head as they closed the shutters and sealed themselves in again.

"It's not as much as we need. We couldn't spare time to check the engine for more masks, either. If we make it through the night, we'll try again in the morning."

Meg gave the hose back to Eric and went to help Jason. Rachel and Rex already had a plywood panel over the doorway to the chief's office and were hammering it in place. Meg and Jason each used a spare boot to carry their hammers and a few handfuls of nails. The punk girl offered to help carry the wood, and so did the mother of the little girl with pigtails.

"Momma will be right back, baby girl. You wait here with Mrs. Cannady, okay? I'll be right back."

The girl sat up close to the older black woman who'd asked about getting medicine.

"You're gonna be fine," Mrs. Cannady said, putting an arm around the little girl's shoulders. "Go ahead, Dayone. Help them keep us safe."

Meg looked at the woman and little girl, and she tried to smile. They both did their best to smile back, and Mrs. Cannady nodded.

The little girl's mother, Dayone, went to the carts and hoisted an armful of 2x4 lumber. Meg joined her and picked up the other end of the boards. When they had the load balanced, they followed the punk girl and Jason up the stairs.

"Thanks for the help," Jason said when they got to the top. The punk girl just nodded and went back downstairs. Dayone offered to help.

"I can go get more wood. Or some nails in case you run out."

"You should rest, conserve your energy. Your daughter needs you," Jason said before Meg could reply. She added her own thoughts as Dayone turned to go.

"Thank you, Dayone. If we need anything, I'll come get you."

The woman gave a nervous wave and went back downstairs.

"We shouldn't ignore their offers, Jason. We might be in better shape physically than most of them, but we need to conserve our energy."

"They're exhausted, and even if they're aren't, I don't think we can expect much out of them."

"Why not? Two of them did just help us, right? And one of them was Little Miss Emo."

"Sure, but most of them…they've never done anything like this. They're the kind of people who expect people like you and me to do everything when the shit hits the fan."

Meg looked at him for a breath before giving up. She didn't have the energy to argue. And she knew he was sort of right.

Sort of.

The survivors *were* all exhausted, and some were probably close to a state of shock. Mental at least. Before they'd come upstairs, Meg scanned the group for signs of infection, but was happy to see a few of them had managed to fall asleep, even with Rex and Rachel hammering down there. The echo of their blows came up the stairs. As she and Jason got to work, Meg tried to keep her hammering as quiet as she could. She hadn't seen any of the monsters outside yet, but daylight was fading.

They got the first set of windows covered before they had to make a trip for more lumber and nails from downstairs.

Jason took a break to use the bathroom first. Meg went downstairs ahead of him and sat on the bottom step. Eric was near the shutters, watching the street. He still had the hose with him, but kept it hanging over his shoulder now. Rex and Rachel were putting the last nails into a double layer of plywood on the chief's office. That left them with one more sheet of plywood. Meg thought about taking it upstairs, but decided it would be better down here.

I hope we have enough to seal this place up for the night.

Over on the cots, Dayone and her daughter were asleep, and Mrs. Cannady looked like she was ready to nod off. Abeer huddled against the wall with her child, but Meg heard the woman's soft cooing. Most of the others were already asleep, or just huddled together and looking scared.

The punk girl was in the corner at the back of the floor angrily swiping at a tablet she had across her knees.

"You've got service?" Meg asked.

"No," the girl said, not looking up.

Meg left it at that. What good would it do? Meg could tell her to get some rest instead of playing some game or whatever the hell she was doing. She could also conserve what little patience she had left.

Might need it soon. We all might.

Jason came down and stepped past her. He went to where Rex and Rachel were finishing up. They exchanged a few words Meg didn't catch. Then Jason wheeled the cart of wood over nearer to the stairs.

"We might need to come back down for more. Closer is better."

Meg grunted a reply. She *was* losing her edge. Patience, hunger, fatigue. It was all settling onto her shoulders and pushing her closer to the floor. She stood up, stretched her arms, and shook herself awake.

"You okay?" Jason asked.

"Yeah. Just running on fumes."

"Ditto," he said, and lifted more two by fours onto his shoulder. Meg grabbed what she could carry and led the way upstairs.

"We'll go next time," Meg said once she and Jason were back upstairs. "Me and Eric. Or Rex. You shouldn't have to take the risk every time."

"What's with Rex anyway? You don't seem to like him much."

That caught Meg off guard. She wasn't used to people she didn't know calling her out that way. Eric got away with it, but he was Eric. And Rex had nothing but clumsy flirting in his bag of tricks.

"He's a probie, and… I don't know. He's not my people I guess."

"We're all each other's people now, aren't we? Probie or not."

Meg paused. It really had come to this. Rex might be the one to save her life. That was always the case, but now it sunk in, and Meg had to accept it.

"Yeah. We are."

They did the rest of the work in silence, except for the banging of the hammers as they drove nails into the two by fours over the last window. They'd created a grid work across the windows in the dorm room. It gave them another layer of protection, and allowed them to look outside without immediately showing themselves to whoever was out there. Meg corrected herself: *Whatever* was out there.

Those things aren't people.

Jason lifted the final two by four into place while Meg drove the nails to hold it against the others. She had one end fixed and was moving to the other when she spotted one of them on top of a car across the street.

"Shit. They're back."

Jason edged back from the side of the window and peered around the boards they'd nailed up. He darted back quickly.

"I don't think it saw us," he said. "Get that end nailed in. Last one and we're done."

Meg hesitated. The first thing Rachel had said when

they came in was that the monsters were attracted to noise.

Thank God they're finished downstairs, otherwise…

"C'mon, Meg," Jason said. "Last one. Let's go."

"It'll hear us. Wait until it leaves."

The thing still sat on the car with its head tilted back, like it was sniffing the air, swiveling its face side to side. Meg couldn't see its eyes or sucker mouth at this distance, but she still had the image in her mind. The fading light cast weak shadows around the monster and made its white flesh even more ghastly to look at.

Should she hammer the nail in? It wasn't even looking at their building. She put a nail to the wood and held the hammer ready. But she couldn't stop looking out the window to watch the thing on the car. It leaped away and scrambled up the building across the street, slinking into a broken window like a trapdoor spider returning to its nest. Meg stared at the window as she lifted the hammer for a swing.

You'll smash your thumb if you don't watch what you're doing. Then you'll scream and make even more noise.

Meg focused on the nail head and swung the hammer.

Bang.

She looked back at the window. The monster hadn't come back.

Bang.

She looked again. Still nothing but a dark empty window. Every window in the building across the street looked just the same. Broken, dark, and empty.

"C'mon," Jason said. "Finish it up."

Bang. Bang.

Something darted away in Meg's peripheral vision. She

couldn't tell if it had come from the building, or if it was just a trick of the light, or her frightened anxious, exhausted mind playing tricks on her. Meg set a second nail to the board and hit it.

Bang.

Meg drove the rest of the nail in with rapid blows, not bothering to look out the window anymore. Jason grabbed the hammer he'd been using and went downstairs ahead of her. Meg hit the nail a final time before looking out the window. Her hand whipped up over her mouth as she backpedaled away and stumbled over the boot they'd carried the nail in. Across the street, at least a dozen of the monsters came scrambling out of the dark windows, leaping onto cars and the fire engine. And stalking their way across the street on a path leading directly to the station house.

Meg whipped around and flew down the stairs two at a time. She nearly bowled Rex over backwards as she descended. He had his gloves on.

"They're at the front door. The locker," he said. Meg heard the scratching and shrieking and it sounded like they were in the chief's office. Rex's face was a mask of panic. A sheen of sweat glistened across his brow and his jaw shook.

"Get it together, man," Jason said. "We need those people upstairs."

A louder banging followed and then a splintering sound. Meg heard Eric's shouting mixed with a rush of water at the front of the app floor. Jason shoved Rex aside. Meg looked at the probie. He shivered, like he was ready to collapse from fright.

"Rex," she said. His eyes moved to meet hers, but she

could tell he wasn't home. "Goddamit."

Meg pushed her way past him as screams echoed through the app floor.

— 20 —

Long Island City, Queens

Jed felt his finger slide from the housing to the trigger on his weapon. They'd made the turn onto Skillman and were going by the rail yards again. Sergeant Boon had let off him for a bit, but he could he the guy back there muttering under his breath in between grunting in pain.

The streets were chill at least. No sign of the monsters anywhere. But just his luck, Jed's side of the truck faced the neighborhood, with its broken windows, cars and trucks smashed together on the sides of the streets. It looked like somebody ran a bulldozer through the neighborhood and just shoved everything that wasn't alive out of the way. The street the convoy had come down was clear, but the farther down Skillman they went, the more Jed realized just how messed up New York had become.

It's like the apocalypse is finally here. Shit's just tore up everywhere.

"Yo, Welch," Boon said. "So you're back in the Corps, huh? You get any of 'em yet? You even seen one of the monsters that did this to me?"

Jed waited a beat before he replied, and he didn't bother answering the sergeant's questions. If Boon was gonna fuck him, he was gonna fuck him, and there was nothing Jed could do about it. So he went with the script whenever a guy gets hurt, figuring it was the safest play he had. "You're gonna be okay, Sergeant," he said.

"Fuck you, Welch," Sergeant Boon said. "I'm gonna' be okay. After they tore my fuckin' hands off. I'm gonna be okay? Fuckin' homie from the damn block. I saw you, Welch. I—"

Jed had looked over his shoulder, out the corner of his eye, and just in time to see Sergeant Boon's eyes roll up as his head lolled over to the side.

"Shit!" Sergeant Kuhn said. He'd turned around and was watching Boon. Jed had his eyes on the dead man, but everyone else seemed to be trying to watch their zone and keep an eye on Boon at the same time.

"Watch your zones, men," Kuhn said. "Sergeant Townsend, we need to remove this body from the truck."

Jed turned around even as he felt Sergeant Townsend coming up the truck bed next to him.

"Get his ankles," Kuhn said.

Jed kept a close eye on Boon's feet. Sergeant Townsend reached down, and as he did, his shoulder brushed against the muzzle of Jed's weapon, which was now aimed at Boon's face.

"Welch, what the fuck?"

"Sergeant!" Jed yelled. Boon's head twitched, then his feet came up off the truck bed as his legs went stiff. He lurched up and screamed as blood leaked from his eyes and nose.

"Get 'em off me! Get 'em off!" Boon yelled, pawing at

the bandages on his hands by slapping them together, like he wanted to scrape them away.

"I can't stop them! Can't—Get 'em off!"

Jed put a round into Boon's chin, just like he'd done with the crazy kid before. Blood spattered out from inside the man's helmet and he fell back onto the truck bed.

"Don't touch it!" Sergeant Kuhn yelled. Everyone else had gone tighter up against the side of the truck, but Sergeant Townsend had moved like he would still get rid of the body. He straightened up and moved back to his position at the rear of the truck.

"Rah, Sergeant," Jed said over his shoulder. He'd gone back to watching the neighborhood as they moved down Skillman.

"Rah?" Sergeant Townsend said, coming up close behind Jed. "You keep your motherfuckin' eyes on your zone. Hear me? Don't turn around now. Just listen. You watch the fuckin' battlefield, son."

Jed just nodded, doing his best to ignore the burn in his cheeks that had come back in force.

He'd hang with this crew until shit went bad, or he saw a way out again. Just like last time. He'd just saved their lives and the best they could do was give him shit. Just like in Boot. Just like Iraq. He lowered his head, wishing he could just jump off the truck right there and get away from all of it. But where would he go, and how would he stay alive with the monsters hiding in every dark corner?

Rainey nudged him then and said something that put his whole world on its head.

"You heard the Sergeant, Welch. Keep your eyes up and on the battlefield."

Jed had a couple words on his tongue and got half of the first one out before Rainey cut him off.

"Corporal. Make sure you say 'Fuck you, Corporal'."

Jed realized he'd never caught Rainey's rank before. He figured the guy for a private like him, maybe a PFC.

Rainey gave him a big shit-eating grin, like he was daring Jed to actually say the words he wanted to say so bad. These guys, though…they wouldn't take attitude from him, not without giving him some serious lumps. But damn it would feel good to just tell Rainey to go fuck himself. He eyeballed the corporal, and Rainey looked like he was ready to start swinging.

Sergeant Townsend put everyone back in line before Jed could dig himself a deeper grave.

"Eyes out, men. You can kiss and make up when we get to Manhattan."

A few chuckles went around the truck, but quieted down just as fast as they'd come.

The neighborhood swept by in front of Jed's tired eyes. His legs still burned from the run, and he felt a nervous shake start in his right thigh.

The truck rolled to a slow stop and Jed snapped out of his thoughts. The remains of a barricade lay scattered across the roadway. Sandbags formed a couple of machine gun positions on either side of the road, but they were all knocked down, like something big had crashed into them. A concrete barrier had been shoved aside, making a path from the opposite lane.

Jed realized they were already at Queens Boulevard.

"We passed Honeywell," he said.

"The fuck are you, a tour guide?" Sergeant Kuhn said. "Eyes damn out, Welch."

Jed let it sink in and join the heat he already felt burning in his gut. These fuckers weren't going to get a damn thing from him. First chance he got, he was gone. He'd take care of himself, just like always. He'd survive, on his own and without anyone around to knock him in the head just because he couldn't make them happy.

The elevated tracks over Queens got Jed thinking differently, though.

They'll just fall on us. Gotta be hiding up there. They'll drop down on top of us.

"Sergeant Townsend."

"The fuck you want, Welch?"

"What if they're hiding up in the tracks?"

"Then we shoot them, Welch."

Sergeant Kuhn leaned around to talk to whoever was in the cab. It didn't take much to guess that was the LT.

Candy ass motherfucker hiding out up there.

"Okay," Kuhn said. "We're doing this fast. We get across the rail yard and then it's a few more blocks to the bridge. You see anything moving, light it up."

The man paused and leaned down to talk to the LT in the cab again. He came back to standing and said, "Back of the truck. Sergeant Townsend?"

"Yeah."

"LT wants you to keep watch over the buses. Give a shout if you see anything going on with them."

"Ain't got much else to be doing," Sergeant Townsend said.

Kuhn grunted and slapped a palm on the truck cab.

"Hold on, men," he said as the truck made the turn onto Queens Boulevard and brought them under the El tracks. Jed couldn't help but shake in his boots as they came fully under the steel girders that supported the train tracks. The truck sped up and he felt his guts clench with fright.

They're gonna drop on us. Gonna fuckin—

And they did. Four of them just flew down out of the metal frame overhead. Jed opened up along with Rainey and the other guy on their side of the truck. He heard gunfire from the other side, too.

The monsters jerked in the air as they fell, landing on the ground in a tangled bloody heap. The truck was still rolling, and Jed was still alive.

"That's how you do it, men," Kuhn said.

Jed flicked his gaze left and right. Rainey looked just about as freaked as Jed felt. The guy to Jed's right was sweating like it was the middle of summer. Or maybe those were tears on his face.

Queens Boulevard raised up in a hump in the middle as they crossed over the rail yards below. A shriek came from behind them. A hollow metallic echo followed, like one of the monsters had landed on top of a bus. Jed wanted to look back to check, but he couldn't take his eyes off his zone. Not for a second. Small arms fire sounded out beneath the El tracks. Tight *pop-pop-pops* and a few seconds of chatter from the SAW up front. The truck and buses kept rolling fast. Jed could see the edge of the rail yards coming up, just empty dirt around scattered rusty piles of metal. A line of trees and bushes separated the mess from the neighborhood on the other side.

They were almost there. Just a little more to go.

Another shriek came from behind them, and then more, like a fucking roomful of the monsters were back there trying to sing a song together.

Jed tried to get a line of sight again, but he didn't dare take his eyes off his zone. Rainey was doing the same thing: looking back the way they'd come and twisting his head back so he could focus on his zone. Jed heard a clattering and scraping overhead. He looked straight up above them and his heart almost flew out of his mouth.

"Shit!" he yelled and lifted his weapon, firing as fast as he could.

A pack of the creatures scrambled and scraped on the El tracks overhead. They moved to keep up with the convoy, leaping and racing along the tracks like a pack of freakish monkeys. Sparks flew off the girders as Jed and the others in the truck tried to shoot the monsters. Some were hit and tumbled onto the street below. But most of the shots missed.

The things seemed to know where to run, like they were keeping covered on purpose.

Jed fired and fired, aiming as carefully as he could while the truck raced down the roadway. He hit one of the monsters and watched it fall to the street where it was crushed beneath the truck tires. Another leaped down several feet in front of the truck and made to jump onto the cab. The man to Jed's right spotted it and pivoted to fire. He got it with a burst to the chest just as another one fell from above and landed on him, taking him out of the truck and to the road below. His screams followed the truck as they rolled on.

Rainey hit Jed in the shoulder with an elbow.

"Eyes out, Welch!"

Jed got back on his game, sending three rounds bursts at anything that moved, but only hitting them when he got lucky. He changed magazines and kept it up. Rainey did the same. Another pack dropped from above, at the far end of the road. The monsters tore down the pavement on all fours, racing at the truck, howling and shrieking as they came. The SAW gunner gave up on fire discipline. The constant pinging of brass on the truck's cab rang in Jed's ears behind the dull hum from the gunfire.

The Ma deuce open up at the back of the convoy, chopping at the air in a steady rhythm.

Jed kept his eyes on his zone, leading the monsters as they raced along the girders, and timing his shots as best he could. The bullets sparked and splattered on the metal. Jed thought he might as well be tossing pennies or pieces of candy, like he was on some kind of fucked up parade float. Then one of the monsters leaped down toward the side of the truck where the other guy had been pulled out. Jed tracked its arc and lit it up with three to the face.

— 21 —

Eric had the hose at full throttle, directing the stream at the side of the plywood Rex and Rachel had nailed up. The monsters were scrabbling to get around the wood that they'd shoved out from the wall. The boards were split down the middle and it was only because Rachel and Jason pushed against them that the monsters hadn't completely broken into the floor.

The survivors had all crowded together at the very back of the floor, in the corner where the punk girl had been sitting. She was wrapped up in a turnout jacket now, and had a mask on. Only her blue hair gave her away.

Abeer, Dayone, and their children, were crowded together around Mrs. Cannady, who stood tall and with her feet firmly planted, like she'd see hell before she let anything happen to the others.

The cots made an obstacle course for anyone wanting to get to them.

Or for them to get out of there.

Meg grabbed a pair of gloves and her axe from where

she'd set them down by the staircase and ran to help Rachel and Jason.

Eric kept his aim on the space the monsters had broken through, and it was working for now. They couldn't get past the stream of water.

Unless they make a bigger hole.

The boards shuddered and Jason nearly lost his footing on the wet floor. Rachel was crouched down beneath him and only just held the boards down as clawed arms occasionally reached through the space, swiping at the air and trying to grab either Jason or Rachel. So far, they'd kept themselves clear by kicking at the arms the instant they came through.

"Axe!" Jason yelled. Meg ran behind Eric and came up to the wall opposite Jason and Rachel's position. The heavy stream of water roared between them, and Eric stepped a little closer to put more force into keeping the things back.

Meg swung down with her axe at the reaching arms and connected with two. Shrieks sounded from behind the boards and the arms retreated immediately. But they were just replaced by more a second later. Meg swung again and missed, slamming the axe into the concrete floor. The blow sent a ringing pain through her hands and she had to fight to keep hold of the axe handle.

The boards shook and creaked again with another blow from the other side. Jason screamed for Rex to bring a hammer and nails.

More arms came reaching through and Meg swung at them, hitting one and taking it off. The thing on the other side roared, and Meg paused with her axe at the ready. She felt guilty for what she'd done, like she'd just maimed a helpless animal.

A second later and she regretted her hesitation as one of the creatures rocketed through the gap in the boards and skittered through the pooling water on the floor. It slid across the floor and to the opposite wall where it quickly scrambled up and twisted its head around to look at Meg. Its ugly yellow eye slits opened and closed and it gave a horrific hiss.

Meg had her axe ready to swing down in case another one came through, but she couldn't take her eyes off the one on the wall. It stared at her with its bloody yellow eyes and popped its sucker mouth, making a disgusting web of saliva in front of its needle teeth.

The survivors screamed at the back of the floor. Jason yelled for Rex to bring the hammer again. Rachel yelled for him then, while Eric kept spraying into the gap in the boards. The thing on the wall moved its gaze from Meg to Eric.

Oh shit!

She moved a second too late. The thing leaped, and not for Eric. It landed on the floor a few feet behind him, and next to the hose. Before Meg could reach it, the monster slashed a clawed hand at the hose and ruptured it.

Water sprayed out as the severed hose went haywire, spinning and flipping like a sea serpent. And the monsters came like a wave through the gap in the boards. Rachel was thrown backwards as the boards bucked and were shoved aside. Two of the monsters crawled in and immediately up the wall beside the boards. Jason reeled away and grabbed an axe off the wall.

Eric backpedalled, dropping the broken hose.

The people at the back of the floor added their screams to the din around Meg. She raised her axe as she approached the one that slashed the hose, but it leaped around her. She tried to pivot and her feet went out from under her on the wet floor.

Meg landed hard on her hip and cried out. She rolled to the side and used her axe handle for support to stand up. When she got to her feet, she nearly fell backwards again. The monster leaped for Eric. He had his arms up, but without a weapon he was a sitting duck. Meg rushed forward and used the axe to shove the monster back toward the boards.

But it was too damn fast.

It sprang forward and tackled Eric, pinning him to the floor.

Behind her, Meg heard Jason and Rachel yelling, and the unmistakable sound of an axe splitting a skull. She raced toward the thing that had Eric. It had one clawed hand holding Eric's head to the floor and with the other it swiped and raked at his coat until it made a hole and reached in.

Eric howled in pain right as Meg reached them and swung her axe into its neck. She shoved it aside and leaned down to help Eric, but he stayed curled up in the fetal position, holding a hand against his ribs. Blood stained his coat and spilled onto the floor, mixing with the water.

"Rex!" Meg yelled. "Trauma bag!"

She turned to see if he'd heard her and felt her throat clench up tight.

One of the things that got in leaped from the wall and tackled Rachel from behind. She'd been helping Jason kill the other one. Jason rushed forward and grappled it. He put his hands around its neck and squeezed. It scraped a clawed hand at his trouser leg and ripped through the material, but Meg didn't see any blood. And Jason didn't let go. He gave a jerk and lifted the thing off Rachel, then swung it around in a headlock and twisted his upper body.

Meg heard a loud crackling sound and looked at the boards, expecting to see more of them coming in. But it was just the sound of Jason snapping the monster's neck. He threw the body away from him. It landed in a heap near the stairs.

A haunted silence spread across the bay. Water trickled and dripped from the walls and across the floor. Eric rolled and groaned beside Meg.

"Rex! Goddammit, bring the trauma bag!"

He was by the hose valve with his hand still on the lever. He must have shut off the water after the monsters got in.

At least he's good for something.

"I'll get it," Jason said.

"Behind the staircase. The cupboard there," Meg told him, pointing.

Jason helped Rachel to her feet and went to retrieve the bandages and other backup gear from the cupboard. He and Rachel had both taken some scrapes. Their turnout suits had rips and tears in places. But Meg didn't see any blood.

While Jason dug through the cupboard for the trauma gear, Rachel grabbed a hammer and some nails off the cart and set to repairing the barricade.

"Eric," Meg said, putting a hand on his shoulder.

"You're going to be all right."

He nodded, and she could see he was holding his face tight against the pain. Whatever the thing had done to him, it had to be serious. His face was pale.

Oh shit, is he turning into one of them?

Meg gripped her axe tighter and held it ready. She couldn't believe it, though, that her best friend was going to turn into…

"Eric?"

"Yeah, Meg. I'm—I'm fine. Losing blood, but—"

He coughed and Meg began to cry. She put her axe down next to him and slowly rolled him to his back. Jason came up beside them with bandages. Meg undid Eric's jacket and carefully peeled it from the wound. Blood flowed steadily from his side. His shirt was one big wet mess, stuck to his skin. Meg ripped her gloves off and snatched up a pair of neoprene ones that Jason had brought. He already had a clean pair on and slapped a compress against Eric's side.

Eric's face went tighter still and he grunted against the pain. Then his legs shook and he whipped his head side to side. Jason kept pressure on Eric's wounds while Meg held her hands on his shoulders.

A thud broke Meg's concentration. She looked to the barricade just as Rachel was thrown backwards and the boards came down on top of her.

— 22 —

Long Island City, Queens

Jed watched the monster fall away from the truck as they sped down the roadway. A few of them were still scrambling around up above, sometimes racing ahead and hanging upside down, like they were taunting Jed and the other guys, daring them to take a shot. Jed did once or twice, and the SAW gunner kept going cyclic every chance he got. Finally Sergeant Kuhn called for a cease fire.

"Wait until they're on the ground or making a jump for us. I think they're testing us, trying to get us to waste ammo."

"You think they're that smart?" Sergeant Townsend hollered up from his position. "I say that's bullshit." Jed turned to see the man scanning the gridwork of steel above them, popping off a round here and there. He hit one, but didn't kill it. The thing just skittered up and around the girders so it was out of view.

"I think—" Sergeant Kuhn started to say, but the SAW gunner opened up and the man's words were lost behind the chatter of gunfire. Another pack of the monsters crawled from beneath the roadway and began pouring over the sides in jumbled piles of pasty white skin and ugly yellow eyes. Jed popped one with a burst to its chest. The SAW gunner lit up the pack on the right side, and Jed heard the guys over there taking shots just like him. Short bursts, quick and clean.

Jed let out a quick sigh of relief when Sergeant Kuhn yelled something and the SAW gunner got his shit under control. Now he just sent bursts at the monsters coming over the sides of the roadway. Jed went between firing at those and trying to pick off the ones that still dropped from above. They'd got most of the ones up there, but a few kept trying to come down on them. Between him and Rainey, though, they'd nearly cleared the monsters off the girders.

"Gonna get 'em, Welch. Gonna get 'em. Yeah!"

Those were the last words Jed heard from the corporal. A monster landed in the truck behind them and everyone seemed to spin at the same time to try and take it out. Two of the guys on the other side of the truck opened up on it, sending a spray of blood into Rainey's face and mouth. He wiped at it and spit. Then he screamed and dropped his weapon and started digging his fingers into his mouth, trying to scrape the blood out.

Sergeant Townsend put a hand on Rainey's shoulder, like he'd hold him together, but Jed threw a butt stroke at Rainey's face, knocking the man backwards and almost out of the truck. He went down on the truck bed and was still spitting and trying to claw his own tongue out.

"The fuck is wrong with you, Welch?" Sergeant Townsend yelled. Jed heard the guys on the other side of the truck still firing and taking out monsters up top. The

SAW gunner was rattling off bursts at the front of the truck. Jed heard Sergeant Kuhn up there shout Townsend's name.

"Your man okay?"

Jed looked down. Rainey had gone still; his eyes were closed and his fingers still jammed into his mouth. Spit and blood covered his lips.

"Welch," Sergeant Townsend said, stabbing a finger into Jed's shoulder.

He looked ready to kill, and he probably would have put Jed down if Rainey hadn't grabbed his lower leg and bit into it. Rainey's face was twisted into a snarl and his teeth dug into the NCO's uniform until they drew blood. Sergeant Townsend screamed and smashed the butt of his rifle at Rainey's face, but he only struck the side of the corporal's helmet.

Another monster dropped from above and landed in the truck, raking its claws down Sergeant Townsend's back as it came down.

Jed watched as the NCO was ripped apart by the thing behind him while Rainey kept grabbing at his legs and trying to bite into them. Sergeant Townsend dropped his weapon and arched his back, flailing as the monster tore into his flesh with its clawed hands.

Shrieks and howls echoed under the El tracks, and the truck still raced forward. Jed brought the butt of his rifle around in an arc and put Sergeant Townsend down and out of the truck. The monster behind him went out, its claws still embedded in his back. They toppled to the pavement and were instantly run over by the bus.

Rainey was lying in the truck bed with a crazed look in his eyes and blood dripping from his mouth. He puckered his lips like he wanted to suck on something.

One of the guys on the other side of the truck shouted at Jed. "Kill it!"

"Go on then," Jed said, lowing the muzzle of his weapon to point at Rainey's face. In the second before Jed fired, whatever was left of the man who used to be Rainey seemed to understand what was happening. He lifted a hand to hold the muzzle of the weapon steady while Jed squeezed the trigger.

Jed shoved Rainey's body off the truck and kicked Sergeant Townsend's weapon out. Blood coated the truck bed and flowed steadily from the wounds in the dead thing that had nearly taken Jed and Rainey out together. Sergeant Boon was just a sack of dead meat underneath it.

The other two guys in the truck were watching the tracks above them. Jed shook himself and did the same. It looked like they'd made it through the worst of it. Nothing else crawled around up there. The SAW gunner had cleared their path from the ones coming over the sides of the road. Sergeant Kuhn nodded at Jed before he told the other two to keep their eyes open. They both acknowledged the order, and Jed had his mouth open to say something. But Kuhn had his back to him already.

***

The convoy rolled through the city, still moving fast as they could. The driver had to slow down to navigate around a mess of tangled up cars at the first intersection after the rail yards. Finally they were into the next neighborhood and following the boulevard out to Queensbridge. They still had to get through a maze of girders and bridges and shit, but Jed knew they'd make it. The things weren't crawling up top anymore. They got through. And that boy on the SAW, he knew how to do it.

At the ramp up to Queensbridge, the bus behind them roared forward and nearly crashed into their truck.

"The fuck?"

Jed waved the driver back. The man flipped him the finger and kept trying to get around the truck.

Abandoned cars up ahead gave them only one lane to use.

"Sergeant," one of the other guys said. Kuhn looked over his shoulder. He slapped a palm on the truck cab and leaned down to shout in the passenger window. They sped up and got through the single lane path. The SAW gunner kept his eyes on the road and Jed tried to do the same on his side of the truck.

But the damn bus kept revving up and coming closer like it was going to ram them.

Sergeant Kuhn leaned down to holler at the LT again. The bus driver picked up a walkie talkie. Whatever he said, it didn't have much effect. Jed's truck stayed at the same speed and would swerve to block the bus when the driver tried to get around them.

"What's that about, Sergeant?" Jed finally asked.

"It's about an asshole who doesn't know when to shut up and do his fucking job. He a friend of yours?"

Mother—

Whatever Jed did to get these guys pissed at him, he was through with it. Fuck 'em. He'd keep an eye out and do his job, sure. And once this truck stopped, he'd move out with a purpose.

159

Just like before. It's the Jed show now, twenty-four seven and three sixty-five.

The truck passed a bunch of industrial places coming up to the river. That's what Jed got to look at anyway. He turned his head to see what was coming up for the guys on the other side of the truck. Nice high rise apartments and some parks and shit. And probably all of it crawling with them things.

A second later, they were on the bridge, on the bottom deck, and it got dark as night around them.

"We got any lights, Sergeant?" one of the other guys asked. Jed was glad he didn't have to open his mouth.

"Just the ones on the front. Eyes out and mouths shut unless you see something."

They crossed over a park right at the river's edge and Jed was looking at some kind of power plant. Two smoke stacks sat quiet and cold next to a yard full of pylons with power lines. Then he spotted the barge in the river hugged up against the edge of the yard like it had run into the shore. Bodies littered the area down there, hanging off the edge of the barge and lying around the yard. Spatters of blood and other shit were everywhere.

He should say something. That's what they'd want him to do, right? Report signs of enemy movement. He had his mouth open, but the bus driver was at it again, and Jed couldn't resist the urge to put the guy in his place. First he threw him the finger with a smile and then he aimed his rifle in the dude's direction.

That got the guy's attention, but not the way Jed wanted to. The bus roared up and came alongside them before their driver could push over and block the lane.

People inside the bus were screaming like crazy and

banging on the windows. Every face was wet with tears, but Jed didn't see any blood.

Sergeant Kuhn shouted something at him, and Jed turned to see the SAW gunner aiming at the bus.

"Get back, Welch. If they're infected, we have to take 'em out."

As the bus passed them, Jed knew the people inside were going to die. Nobody looked infected, at least not that he could tell. They all still looked human anyway. But at the back of the bus, the emergency exit was open, and a spray of blood coated the inside of the door.

"Shit," Kuhn said.

The SAW gunner followed with a question. "Where's their marshal?"

"Marshall?" Jed asked.

"The guy with the LAW rocket. He's supposed to be at the back of the bus in case anyone inside is infected."

"In case?"

"He takes the infected person down," Sergeant Kuhn said. "Or takes them all down if he has to."

Jed couldn't believe it. They'd had a guy in there with a fucking LAW rocket to put the whole bus down just in case—

A spray of blood coated the windows inside the bus, and then another. A guy in a Yankees hat was leaning up against the glass coughing out blood. He tried holding his ball cap on as he started shaking and spitting all over the place. A lady a few seats back was doing it, and then another guy. They were all sitting near the back of the bus.

The SAW gunner went to work and Jed felt his world fall apart.

Those are people. They're not all infected.

The bullets kept flying into the bus. The gunner aimed for the ones that were going all crazy first. A couple of people ran for the back of the bus. Sergeant Kuhn dropped them before they got to the door. Everyone else was up at the front. The driver tried to get them away, but the SAW gunner shifted his aim and then the bus went off to the side, grinding against the concrete divider and sending sparks all over the place until it screeched to a stop up against a wrecked pick up truck.

— 23 —

Meg had her axe in her hand as soon as the barricade fell away from the wall. One of them sat crouched in the doorway staring at her. It was much bigger than any of them she'd seen so far. This one looked like it might have been a boxer or a wrestler when it was human. Thick veins crossed its pale white skin. And blood stained its sucker lips and clawed hands.

Rachel shoved the boards up so she could roll out from under them just as another creature came in behind the first. They seemed to trade looks. Meg couldn't believe it.

They're communicating?

Jason rolled under Meg's guard and came up beside her. He helped Rachel to her feet and they both lifted their axes from where they'd set them down. For a tense moment, Meg and the others faced off with the monsters through the doorway.

The big one leaped straight for Meg. She swung as it flew toward her, but her aim was off. The axe head slid off the thing's shoulder, barely slicing into its flesh. It rolled away from the blow and came up in a crouch against the shutters.

Meg heard Jason and Rachel shouting behind her.

The one in front of her made a hesitant step forward. Meg held her axe across her body, ready to swing or shove the thing if it came for her.

It tilted its head and let out a hiss, then a fast shriek.

Jason shouted from Meg's right, but she didn't dare turn to look. She heard axes impacting on bodies and sometimes the wall or floor. Rachel yelled, and Meg finally caught what they were saying.

"Rex! Help!"

The one in front of Meg tilted its head upward and sniffed. That's when she recognized it. This was the one from outside, the one she'd seen when she was nailing the barricade together upstairs.

Is it the leader? My god, do they have leaders?

She stepped forward, passing by Eric's still and silent body. He was dead. They'd been too late and he lost too much blood.

She'd be damned if she'd go down without getting some revenge.

Meg readied herself for the leader to charge her. But it seemed to be waiting for her to make a move, like it wanted to give her a chance before it killed her.

"Well fuck you, too, then," Meg said. She gritted her teeth and raised her axe for a swing right as she heard the sound of shattering glass from upstairs.

Shit!

The leader jerked its head up and shrieked again. Meg swung as it was lowering its head. She thought she saw a

164

hint of recognition it its yellow slit eyes just as her axe came down into its skull.

Meg wrenched her axe out of the monster's shattered head and spun to take in the floor behind her. Rachel and Jason had the doorway covered, taking turns swinging axes at the monsters as they tried to get in. They held them off pretty well, but eventually one would get up onto the wall and crawl along the ceiling, out of reach of the axes.

If they could get another hose connected…

Rex shifted from one foot to the other at the back of the bay, in front of the survivors. He had an axe in his hands and looked at the staircase. One of the monsters had come down, and sat crouched on the bottom step. It turned its head around halfway, looking at the dead one Jason had thrown there. As the new one turned its head and rolled its shoulders, a sickening echo of cracks and pops came into the bay. Then the monster leaped out and raced along the floor to the far wall. Meg watched Rex track its movement, turning to face it as it hung on the wall and approached him and the survivors.

"Rex!" Meg shouted just as another one launched from the stairs and landed in the middle of the survivors.

Screams and shrieks echoed around the room. Meg raced for the end of the app floor. If Rex could hold them off—Meg cringed inside as she watched Rex swing his axe half-heartedly. The one that jumped into the survivors was tearing people apart and all Rex could do was back up against the wall beside the stairs.

Another one came down the steps just as Meg got there. She missed with the first swing and had to swing upward quickly. Her second blow landed, and caught the thing in its throat. Blood sprayed out, covering Meg's face shield.

Screams and cries of pain surrounded her. Meg swiped at her shield with her jacket sleeve. That only smeared the blood. She could see better, but still not good enough to fight.

"Rex! Help them!" she screamed. Somewhere nearby she heard someone grunting, like they were fighting. She had to hope it was Rex and that he'd finally grown a spine.

Jason roared from somewhere behind Meg. She spun in time to see him swinging his axe into another big creature, like the leader Meg had killed before. It fell to the ground with the axe in its chest. Blood poured from the wound as Jason yanked on the axe handle to dislodge his weapon. Rachel had her back to him and swung her axe back and forth to fend off two of the things that crawled from the doorway along the walls.

Meg wiped at her face shield as she ran to help Rachel. She could see enough to swing now and brought her axe down on a monster's head. Rachel bashed the other one with the flat of her axe, knocking it from the wall. It reared up to strike when Rachel swung back to sink the blade into its face.

Meg wiped a glove down her face shield over and over until her vision was clear. She had a good view now. The app floor was a bloody mess. She heard people behind her cowering, whimpering, and sobbing. Rex was still near the remaining survivors. The one that leaped into them had taken down Abeer and her child. They lay on the floor in a heap next to the pink sweater lady and at least five others. Dayone and the punk girl were alive, though, and hid in the corner with the remaining survivors. Dayone's little girl cowered behind them all.

"Where's Mrs. Cannady?"

Rex to a step to his left, revealing the woman lying on her back with her blouse covered in blood.

"It moved too fast," he said. "I couldn't—"

"*Meg!*" Rachel yelled.

Meg turned in time to see Eric staggering across the floor toward the other two firefighters.

He launched himself at Rachel and tackled her. Jason moved fast, knocking Eric aside, but he rolled with the blow and got his legs under him just as Rachel jumped to her feet. She and Jason held their axes ready and circled around so they had Eric from both sides. His face was already changing. His lips pushed out and he made a sucking motion with his mouth.

Eric reared back and lifted his face to the ceiling to scream. Then he doubled over and began gnawing on his own arm.

"Eric!" Meg called to him. He lifted his head and looked at her. She watched as his eyes narrowed and yellowed, with blood leaking from them. Jason and Rachel approached him, ready to strike. But Eric flicked his head to the side, eyeing them. He dropped to all fours and scrambled away from their swinging axes.

More shrieks and howls came from the doorway as another group of the creatures raced into the chief's office. Jason filled the doorway and swung like a man possessed. His axe moved in a blur, left and right, and blood spattered into the app floor with every strike.

Rachel went after Eric, tracking him along the far wall. Meg wanted to join her, to help.

They both need me. But Eric—What the hell is happening?

Eric had gotten around Meg on the wall while she stared at him, tears dripping from her nose and chin.

"Meg," Rachel said, prodding her in the shoulder with her fist. "You need to kill it. That's not Eric anymore. That's not your friend up there."

He was getting closer to the back of the floor now. Meg and Rachel moved with him, axes up. They had to kick the cots aside to reach the area where the survivors were hiding. When they were only feet away from the survivors, a scream to Meg's left startled her and she had to move her attention from Eric.

Some of the people who had been attacked were standing up as monsters. Three of them were up on their knees with blood streaming from their eyes. Their fingers curled into claws as they pulled and then tore at their own skin.

Mrs. Cannady was hunched over like a grotesque football player hell bent on killing anything that got in her way.

Rex finally got his axe over his head and managed to swing down into Mrs. Cannady's back before she could step toward Dayone and the others. The punk girl pressed herself back against the people behind her. Dayone's little girl grabbed her mother's hand. Their screams were agony in Meg's ears.

The moment stretched out for Meg. She couldn't move even as she heard Rachel yelling at her. In that instant, Eric leaped from the wall, tackling the punk girl.

He brought her down in a tangle and Meg's knees buckled as she watched Eric tear into the girl. The others who had changed rushed into the mass of survivors, clawing and ripping their way through them. Rex used his axe to swat at some, but he'd landed his only effective blow of the day. All he managed to do was redirect the monsters' attacks onto other people.

Rachel screamed as she raced into the crowd, smashing two of the monsters in the head with a single swing. Jason gave a monstrous roar behind them and Meg turned in time to see him finish off the last ones in the chief's office. He stepped back, arms shaking and his axe hanging down to scrape the floor. Jason staggered back a step and Meg worried he'd been infected. But he'd only slid his foot through the blood and water on the floor.

"Jason!" Rachel yelled. Meg snapped her attention back to see Rachel was surrounded by three of them.

And the people…

Dayone?

They were all dead. All of them. Cut down by Eric and the others who had turned. It had taken only seconds.

Rex had backed himself into the opposite corner and faced off against one of them. Rachel swung at one and caught it in the head, but that left her open for the others. Eric and three more were crawling on the walls above them, flicking their tongues out of their horrific mouths.

They move so fast. I can't—I can't.

You're good, Meg. You're good.

Lurching to her feet, Meg stepped up to stand beside Rachel. Jason tore through the cots to join them. They stood with their backs together, axes out and ready. Meg kept her eyes on Eric. He kept looking at the people on the ground at Meg's feet. She risked a glance at Dayone and her little girl. They'd both been bitten, and blood welled from Dayone's throat. She held a hand over the wound, but Meg knew it was hopeless. The girl was only bleeding from a bite on her shoulder, but already showed symptoms of the infection.

Meg's heart broke over and over again. A hiss from the wall above her tore her attention away just in time. Eric leaped down to land in front of her, blocking her view of Dayone and her girl.

"I'm sorry, Eric."

She swung and put the blade of her axe into his skull, dropping him to the floor. Beside her Rachel did the same to another one that had leaped down beside Eric.

Jason's shouts filled the bay and she turned to see him taking out the last two that were mobile, including the one that had Rex pinned in the corner.

Dayone died as Meg got to her. She went down on her knee and put a hand on the woman's shoulder. Dayone's face shook as blood began leaking from her eyes.

"My gir—"

And then she was gone, shuddering as the virus consumed her.

Meg felt a hand on her back. It was Rachel.

"Let me. You help Jason get the barricade fixed."

Meg fell backwards onto her hip. Her axe slipped from her hand and clattered to the floor beside her. She closed her eyes, but she couldn't block the sound of Rachel's axe as the woman ensured no more monsters would rise from the bodies in the corner.

— 24 —

Long Island City, Queens

Jed kept his weapon up and stared at the ruined bus as they came up beside it. The truck slowed down and the SAW gunner had his weapon up and ready. Jed copied the guy, keeping his rifle aimed at the bus. But his finger refused to touch the trigger. Jed saw some movement, a man crawling out of a busted window with his hands up. He screamed that he was all right, that he wasn't infected.

But Jed saw the blood leaking out of the man's eyes.

"Take him out, Welch!" Sergeant Kuhn ordered.

Jed couldn't do it. Couldn't even shoot to put someone out of his misery. The guy wasn't a monster yet.

All them people. They weren't infected. They weren't—

The SAW gunner lit up the bus and the man in the window toppled backwards as the bullets tore into him. Jed fired then, snapping two rounds into the bus at two other people moving around in there. He didn't know if they were infected or not. But they'd have to be if the first guy was.

They had to be. Right? They had to be.

Sergeant Kuhn mumbled something up at the front of

the truck, but Jed didn't catch it. He was too busy hating what he'd just witnessed.

The guys on the other side of the truck both grunted. "Looks like they're gone, Sergeant," one of them said.

"So you want to take a nap? Eyes out, goddammit."

Least it's not just me getting shit on.

The truck sped up and they left the bus behind. They were halfway across the bridge now, and moving fast again. Wrecked cars sat scattered on the road in places, up against the concrete barrier. A little Miata was halfway off the bridge on the right side up ahead. Jed wanted to see if anyone was in the car, but they passed by it too fast, and he had to keep his attention up top and on the left side.

One of the things chewed on a body inside a car on the other side of the road. Then Roosevelt Island went under them and was gone just as fast. Jed figured he should say something about the one in the car, and the ones moving on Roosevelt Island and climbing the bridge towers that they passed. But his mouth wouldn't work. His tongue felt like a dry hunk of stone in his mouth when he thought about the people in the bus.

They just killed them all. We did. We killed them all.

***

Queensboro Bridge, Manhattan

The convoy made it across the bridge and Jed could see the sky approaching through the grillwork cage that covered the bottom deck of the bridge. Up ahead the top deck split into two separate roads on either side of the cage. Jed didn't see anything moving up there. Nothing crawling in the dark. No shadows jumping from the road above. He still caught his breath each time they passed under the metal beams that crossed overhead.

One.

Two.

Three.

Four.

And then they were under the fading sunlight again. The sky came through the cage in weak streams, but enough that Jed could see their truck clearly.

Streaks of blood and gore seemed to cover every surface. The bodies behind him were covered in bright red pools of infected blood that had begun to go dark at the edges. The seat to his left and right was smeared with blood. It was like he occupied the only clean spot on the truck.

Sergeant Kuhn hollered at him to keep his eyes out, and Jed did what he was told.

When the NCO slammed his hand on the truck cab, and the truck slowed down hard, Jed had to look. What he saw put him on the back foot quicker than shit.

The road up ahead was jammed tight with a tangle of cars and trucks. The bottom deck of the bridge emptied onto a four-lane exit ramp that dropped back down to street level. The ramp was a fucking mess. Shit everywhere. Sandbags all over the place spilling out or just in the way. Cars rolled up on their side, some slammed tight against the barrier beside the road, crushed between the concrete and a bigger vehicle.

There's gotta be people in them.

As they got closer, Jed noticed the people in the cars. They'd all been shot. Most of the cars were just wrecked, smashed to shit. Pebbles of window glass covered the street. But the ones that still had windshields…they all had bullet holes in the glass, and the people inside didn't look like they'd been infected. Someone had shot them all, just like the guy on the SAW did to the bus. It was like killing the disease was more important than helping people who weren't infected yet.

This ain't how it's supposed to be. Ain't what I signed up to do.

Their truck came to a stop and Sergeant Kuhn told them all to dismount. The SAW gunner and the guys on the other side all hopped out quick. Jed hesitated one second too long. Before he knew it, Sergeant Kuhn had him by the LBE and was dragging him off the truck.

"I can get down myself!" Jed hollered once they were on the ground and his had his feet under him.

"You can? Really? Okay. Can you take some fucking orders? What about showing some respect for rank? Or—Goddammit, Welch!"

Sergeant Kuhn stormed off around the truck. Jed heard the cab door open. The SAW gunner and the other two guys had climbed down and were holding positions near the bus.

"Man, fuck this," Jed said. He stepped back from the truck and made sure the guys by the bus weren't looking at him. They had their attention on the bridge and Sergeant Kuhn was who knew where, so Jed stepped back once more, ready to bolt. He went to turn when he felt a gun against his back.

"You want to get in line, soldier."

The pressure of the gun went away. Jed looked over his shoulder. A brown dude stood next to Sergeant Kuhn. Jed couldn't figure the guy for Mexican or something else, but he looked a lot like Chips. Same round face and little bit of fuzz on his top lip. Jed had to shake himself when he looked the man in the eyes.

But he couldn't be Chips.

Chips is dead. He shot himself in his kitchen. He's dead.

This guy was wearing an ACU, carrying an M16 in one hand and a 9mm in the other. He had a butter bar tab on his uniform. Jed slowly came to half attention, but he kept his eyes on the LT while the man holstered the 9mm.

"Your weapon, soldier," the man said, and motioned with his eyes at Jed's M16. He hadn't even realized that he'd brought it up and at the ready.

"Yes, sir," Jed said, relaxing and lowering the muzzle to aim at the ground.

"I'm putting you on point, Welch," the LT said. "Trade with Cory on the SAW for now."

The SAW gunner came up to Jed and lifted the ammo bags he had strapped around him. Jed took those, and then traded weapons with him.

"You're Cory?" Jed asked as he strapped on the ammo bags and slung the weapon at the ready.

"Corribol, motherfucker. The name's Corribol." The guy grunted while he checked over the M16. "The fuck you do to this thing?"

"One of them did it. Threw it across the street."

"Enough talk," the LT said. He motioned for Jed to join him and Sergeant Kuhn by the truck. They had a map out. The LT held it against the side of the truck and used a pen to trace their route. Jed recognized the city grid laid out clear enough, but didn't none of it look like what was all around them.

"Welch, I need you to find a path through this shit up here and establish a zone of fire on the other side. Sergeant Kuhn will guide the civilians down to the street. The other men will maintain our perimeter here. We're taking them one bus at a time. Rally point is Columbus Circle, other side of Central Park. We go down 60th to the park, then follow 59th along the edge."

It was a second before Jed put it together.

"We—We're doing it on our own, sir?"

"That's right, Welch. Me, you, and Corribol. Sergeant Kuhn and his men will hold position with the bus until we get back."

"What about our driver, sir? Or the HMMV?"

"Driver? You're looking at him, Welch. Hummer got ate up on the bridge."

Jed looked down the side of the bus. He could see the second one behind the first. But he didn't see the Hummer anywhere. Jed looked back at the LT and nodded.

"Yes, sir."

Sergeant Kuhn traded a look with the LT, then told his men to take positions at the front and rear of the first bus. The second bus drove down beside the first so the door was in between the two vehicles. The doors opened on both buses and two soldiers stepped out carrying LAWs and M16s.

The marshals. Right.

Jed thought about asking if they were coming with them, but they'd already moved out to the rear of the vehicles.

Fucking rear guard duty. About as safe as being on point.

"Remember your fire discipline," Corribol said. He

was off to the side, by their truck and with the LT. Jed was ready to give the guy some shit for losing his cool back on the bridge and going cyclic, but he kept his tongue.

"Move out, Welch," the LT said.

Jed gave a quick nod, lifted the SAW as best he could, and looked for the easiest way to climb over the pile of ruined cars and bodies that blocked their path.

— 25 —

Upper East Side, Manhattan

The pounding of a hammer snapped Meg from a daze. She'd nearly passed out from exhaustion. Jason and Rachel were repairing the barricade over the chief's office. Rex was nowhere to be seen. But the shutters were partly cracked.

"Where's Rex?" Meg asked, scrambling for her axe and coming up on her knees with the weapon in her hands.

"He's out there," Jason yelled back. He held the last plywood sheet while Rachel hammered it in place.

"Why is Rex outside? What did you do?"

"We didn't do anything!" Rachel hollered back. She stared Meg down through her face shield, eyes wild and angry. She still had the hammer in her grip, and Meg thought for a second the woman would charge her.

"So why is he—"

"Like I said. We didn't do anything. Just like he didn't do anything. Not a damn thing at all, did he? So he grew a pair and went out to get more masks from the engine."

Meg rose up and walked to the end of the bay, crouching as she got close to the shutters.

She jerked backwards and nearly stumbled when Rex's head and upper body came under the door in a rush. He had a bundled up turnout coat that he threw inside as he scooted forward on his stomach. As soon as his feet were in, he lurched up and raced for the chain to lower the door.

Meg watched it all in disbelief. Rex Finney, the paranoid probie? Go out on his own to get extra masks?

"I got two more," he said, looking at Jason and Rachel. They both nodded, and Jason stooped to pick up the jacket Rex had thrown in.

"I didn't see any of them, and the rest of the gear…it had blood on it. I didn't touch it."

"I'm sure you didn't," Jason said. He pulled two masks from the jacket and handed one to Rachel.

"The others were all ruined in the fight. These are the last two good ones we have."

Before Meg could say anything, Jason and Rachel removed their face shields and strapped on the masks.

So the lines have been drawn. Fine.

"I'll go upstairs then," Rex said. "If that's all right."

Jason waved his hand at Rex like he wanted him to just go away, and then he paused to give the man some marching orders.

"Grab a hammer this time, and make sure those windows are blocked off all the way."

Meg was about to say something, but Rex had already taken off for the stairs. He skipped around the dead bodies, snatched up a hammer and some nails from the cart, and disappeared up the steps a moment later.

"I thought we were all each other's people now."

No replies greeted Meg's attempt at fixing the situation, only the banging of hammers as Jason and Rachel laid the last of their 2x4s across the plywood barrier. Whatever had gone down between Rex and the others, Meg was clearly being left out of it.

She stared at the blood and the bodies, feeling her mind slowly falling apart.

Nobody should have to see this much death. Not even in war. This is why we shouldn't have war.

Meg felt herself closing down. She heard her grandmother's words in her mind, but they were empty of any love or encouragement she used to feel. Now all she had was purpose. A blind reason to keep going.

Survival. That's all we have left to us.

"We need to clean it up," Jason said from behind her. She turned to see him aiming a hammer at the bodies in the corner.

"I'll take care of it," Meg said. "You and Rachel get a new hose on the valve and spray the place down. We can crack the shutters enough to wash it all outside."

"I'll help you with the bodies," Rachel said.

"No. I'll do it myself."

Rachel flipped a hand in the air as if to say *Whatever.*

Meg hung her axe on the rack and went to the basement door. She opened it, feeling the cold draft rise up from below. It would function as a morgue for a few days and might keep the smell down a bit. They could close the door, and seal it up with blankets around the cracks.

Do we have a few days? If they get in again…

***

Meg set Dayone's little girl between her mother's body and Mrs. Cannady's. Abeer and her infant were on the other side of the basement space, up against the wall where the cots were usually stacked. The punk girl and pink sweater lady were next. Meg cursed herself for not ever learning their or the other women's names, or their children's.

There had to be other survivors out there somewhere. Other parents and their children. Mothers and fathers. Uncles and aunts. Grandparents. All of them. She couldn't save these people, but she'd save someone. Somewhere in this city there was a person Meg would help stay alive.

She got up on her feet, and slowly made her way down the basement steps. After a dozen more trips like that, she had all the bodies moved. Jason and Rachel had taken the cots and stacked them out of the way. They'd put a new hose on the valve and were ready to spray down the walls and floor of the bay.

"I'll be up in a minute," Meg told them. She went down the basement steps, ignoring Rachel's look. The woman seemed like she wanted to apologize, or maybe just tell Meg to stay with them in case more of the monsters came back.

But Meg had something to do first.

In the basement, she paused by each body and said a quiet farewell to the person. If she knew the names, she spoke them. When she didn't, she said she was sorry. She knew there was something important to do for Abeer and her baby, but Meg didn't know the ritual and she felt it would be disrespectful to do it wrong or only halfway.

Who would know?

She would. And that had to be enough for now. If she was going to get through this, she had to trust her heart and mind together.

"I'm sorry, Abeer. Sorry I couldn't do more for you. For any of you," she said, turning in a circle and looking at them all lying there. Then she went upstairs.

Rachel was waiting at the door when she came up.

"We can't clean the place until this door is closed."

Meg thought about it for second and nodded. Silently, she collected blankets and, with Rachel's help, covered the gaps around the basement door. When they were done, Jason began the grisly task of spraying down the bay. Rachel and Meg cracked the shutters just enough to let the mess out onto the street.

When the water ran clear, Jason shut off the nozzle. They waited in silence, staring at the dripping walls. Meg looked at all the wet posters and photographs now splotchy and stained. The group photographs that she was in hung lower on the wall than the others, being some of the newer ones. The frames were cracked and the glass broken in almost all of them.

Spare axes and turnout coats lay scattered against the walls. The stack of cots dripped water and, as Meg watched, slowly slid down the wall until they tumbled into a heap of sticks and wet canvas.

It looked like a bomb had gone off in the app floor.

"We should close the shutters," Rachel said at last.

"Yeah."

Meg reached for the chain and slowly put the door

back down. She thought about heading upstairs to crash in the engineer's room, but she paused. A crackling sound came to her ears from outside. Meg panicked and raced away from the shutters.

"What is it?" Jason yelled up to her. "Are they back?"

"Yes. I—No. No! That's gunfire! There's someone out there!"

— 26 —

Jed was thinking he'd picked the right job after all. Being up on point, he might be the first to get it. But it'd be over quick at least. Except he didn't see it happening like that. Not with that big chain of civilians all lined up behind him.

The LT was the second man in line, with the civilians teamed up in groups of three behind him. Corribol was at the rear with Jed's M16. They staggered their movement, leap-frogging the civilian groups down the blocks. Sometimes Jed would see movement in a skyscraper, but he could never be sure. Everything looked like flashes of pale flesh in the fading afternoon light. But it was quiet, and since nothing was jumping out and tearing him up, it seemed like they'd make it out okay. Just a few more blocks to go and they'd be at the rally point. Central Park was right up ahead.

A series of shrieks put Jed up against the wall of the nearest building. He had the SAW up, but the damn thing was heavy, and he needed to find a support for the bipod fast. A taxi was up on the curb just a little ways back, but the LT was already there with the first group of civilians. Corribol had the other groups running to catch up.

Jed jerked his head left and right, then up, over and over again. No way was he going to let them sneak up on him. Not when he had a SAW in his hands.

Goddamn zombies. Monsters. Shit, I don't care what you are. You are not getting Jedediah Monroe Welch today.

He spotted them as they launched from the second floor of the skyscraper he had just passed, the one next to the LT's position. Corribol and the other civilians had just come up to join the LT's group. At least a dozen of the monsters jumped from the broken windows and straight down onto the LT, Corribol, and the civilians. Screams and shouts and gunfire mixed to shatter the weird silence that had taken over New York City.

For a moment, Jed just watched it happen. The monsters biting and ripping with their claws. People screamed and fell to the sidewalk. The LT shot one just as another leaped onto him from the building. Corribol had two of them down before he was taken out by another pair jumping from the windows.

Jed swallowed the scream that was building. The horror and screams faded in his ears as he felt the SAW bucking in his hands.

The LT went down, then the first few civilians. Jed was doing them a favor. The monsters had jumped right on them, and Jed saw the LT get bit. Tears flowed fast and hot down Jed's face, but he kept firing. Burst after burst put the monsters down, thrashing and clawing at the bullet holes peppering their chests. Finally, Jed went cyclic and sprayed the mass of writhing bodies, monsters and victims alike. He could have let them live, but they'd have been killed later anyway. Or turned into monsters themselves.

Corribol was already twitching on the ground when Jed put a burst into the soldier's chest.

This is what you did. You protected yourself, so I'm just doing the same thing now.

Jed let up for a second, scanning the bodies down the street. A few of them moved, then Jed realized they were the monsters, sucking on the people they'd just killed.

Jed fired again until he didn't see anything moving.

Anything that wasn't Jed Welch was as good as dead. But Jed didn't feel much alive inside of himself either.

I gotta get out. Gotta go. Get out of here. Get safe. Free. Away.

He didn't even know he'd been running until he came up short against a concrete barrier. Someone shouted to him from his left and he spotted a soldier with a weapon standing inside a smashed up storefront.

"Yo, c'mon. Get on in here. You got ammo for that SAW?"

Jed ducked around the busted glass and stepped over the ruined window display. The guy who'd called him into the store was a black dude, thin like a beanpole and with a goofy grin stretched across his mouth. "My name's Bree," he said, holding out a hand. Jed ignored it and just jutted his chin at the guy as he came inside.

He still felt dizzy from killing the monsters.

And the people.

Jed stumbled into the store and nearly tripped over a mannequin wearing a purple blouse and those short shorts Jed used to like so much. Looking at them now didn't make him feel anything, though.

"We callin' her Hoeisha," Bree said, laughing like any

of the nervous tweakers Jed used to run with. He kept the SAW up close to his belly, out of instinct. Something about the soldier in front of him didn't sit right. Jed sniffed and wiped a hand under his nose fast before grabbing the SAW again and holding it tight.

"Welch," he said.

"Welch. Cool, man, cool. Like I said, I'm Bree. Back here I got Marks, Sharpe, and Hardly."

"The name's Harney," another soldier said with a drawl that reminded Jed of home. A trio of guys were hanging out behind the cash register. The guy named Harney was a white dude like Jed. Could have been from Georgia himself, but definitely down south somewhere. The other two, Marks and Sharpe, were probably New Yorkers all their life. Some kind of mixed race guys, skin that looked like it might be brown or maybe it was just the shadows, Jed couldn't tell. All four of the guys had M16s and held them by the butt stocks or carry handles, almost like they didn't have a use for them anymore.

Jed stepped deeper into the shop and turned to face the window, holding the SAW across his chest. "Who y'all with?"

"We ain't *with* nobody," Bree said. "Less you mean ourselves. We what's left of the *four-oh-one*," Bree said. "Got chewed the fuck up on Queens Boulevard. Barely made it over the bridge and didn't get more'n three blocks. Bunch of civilians cramming up the roadway there, trying to get out of Manhattan."

"We told 'em this was the safe zone," Harney said.

"Yeah, and did they listen? Nope," said one of the other guys. Jed didn't know if it was Marks or Sharpe, but he didn't much care right then. Bree had a look in his eye that told Jed they'd done something like he had. Run off probably.

Or maybe these are the guys who shot all those people in the cars? Why would they do that, unless...

Jed figured he should say something, anything to keep cool with these guys. If they'd bailed out like he had, that was one thing. He'd even understand if they'd had to shoot people to keep from getting infected themselves. But if they'd gone mustang and just started shooting people for the hell of it...

Jed moved farther into the shop, away from the window and a little ways farther from Bree. Something about the guy's face told Jed that Bree wasn't being straight about everything. And he got a sick feeling in his gut that he shouldn't have come into the storefront in the first place.

Only one way to find out. Get 'em talkin' and see what they say.

That had been his dad's rule about people, the only thing Jed had to remember the man by.

"What's the plan? Shit's fucked up out there."

"Yeah, I'd heard," one of the New York guys said. Dude was tall, like Bree, and had a funny looking nose, like on those old puppets made out of paper and painted all kinds of colors. He had big lips and a lazy right eye that pointed off to the side of his face.

"C'mon now, Marks," Bree said. "Man's just in out of the storm. Got that SAW, too."

Jed caught it that time. Bree kept eyeing the SAW, and he got a hungry look in his eyes when he mentioned it. Jed held the weapon up tighter and let his finger go loose around the trigger guard so he was ready to fire if he had to.

"I was with the 401st," he said. "We had some civvies in a bus back there at the bridge. But we couldn't get into Manhattan on the trucks. Bunch of cars were all smashed together there. Some people got shot just driving. I figure they must have been infected or something. You see that when you came through?"

"Nah," Bree said quick. "Must've been right after we got over the bridge. Told you all them civilians was driving out of Manhattan. Bet that was them."

If Bree was holding wild cards in his hand, he was playing better than Jed ever had. He still couldn't figure if the guy was being straight with him or not. Something was up with the dude, and Jed felt like time was running out to get the truth. Daylight was fading, and he did not want to be stuck in a ruined storefront with these guys over night.

"Rally point was supposed to be up here somewhere, wasn't it?"

Bree gave him a look and Jed figured it out in half a beat.

Supposed to be.

A lot of shit was *supposed to be* for Jed when he got back to New York City. But watching a damn zombie plague eat the place alive wasn't part of the bargain. Getting stuck with a bunch of dirtbags wasn't much better.

"So we just chilling here? What are we doing?"

"We're fucking dying, dude," Marks said.

"Yeah," Sharpe added. "Maybe you didn't see it, but the city's fucked. The Army's fucked. The Marines are fucked. I guess the Navy's all right, but that's because the fucking squiddies are out on their boats. Not here in the shit waiting for a damn zombie to jump on their ass and start slamming away like it's fucking prom night."

"Dude, will you *please* shut up," Harney said. "I've had about enough of your mouth."

"Yo," Bree cut in on the fight before it got started. "Keep that shit in your pants 'til you find a toilet."

"So you're in charge now?" Jed asked.

"Yeah," Bree said.

Jed hadn't spotted his rank before, and he didn't see any on him now. His tab was missing. Guy was probably bullshitting, but the other dudes weren't up in arms about it.

The echo of gunfire from out on the street rattled into the storefront, putting every man on alert. Jed stayed to the side, but kept the SAW up. A flash of movement in front of the store startled him and he sent a burst out through the broken remains of the window. Glass shattered and pinged off the other shards already on the shop floor.

"Cease fire! Cease fire!" someone yelled from outside. "Friendly!"

Bree was up close to Jed and put a hand up for him to cease fire. "Yo, hold up with the SAW, Welch. Hold up. Save that ammo." Bree went forward with his rifle at the ready. He called out, "Hey, who's out there? We *four-oh-one*. Civil Affairs."

"US Marines. Lance Corporal Maloof. I got three guys with me. We're coming in."

Jed lowered the SAW as the four Marines came into the storefront. They managed to get in without tripping over the mannequin. Bree greeted the first guy to come in. He said he was Maloof, and he introduced the other men.

"Pinzler, Tracy, and Stevens."

They were all white dudes. Maloof gave a few words of command and the three Marines formed a perimeter at the front of the shop. They lifted their weapons and scanned the area, taking in every inch of the scene. One of them stayed facing out to the street, roving his muzzle back and forth while the other two switched between watching the street and watching Bree and his guys.

"The rally point is moved two blocks away," Maloof said. "There's a fire station there that's supposed to have survivors. We just got word from your actual on that."

"You got radio to them?" Bree asked.

Maloof nodded and patted a mic slung over his shoulder.

Jed didn't miss the cagey look that went over Bree's face.

I bet these guys did do something really fucked up to get away back on the boulevard. Like worse than running away fucked up.

"We're heading to the fire station," Maloof said. "Who's in charge here?"

He looked at Jed when he asked the question, but Bree spoke up before Jed could say anything.

"That's me."

"You're an NCO."

"Yeah, E-4. Corporal."

Maloof didn't buy it, that was clear. And Jed didn't either. Bree might be E-4, but he was a Specialist at best.

"Who do you want on point, Corporal?" Maloof asked, and Jed could see he was fucking with Bree, trying to catch him out. When Bree didn't answer right away, Maloof saved them all the trouble.

"We'll put Stevens up front. Your squad can take the

middle, *Corporal.* Me and my guys'll cover the rear. Stevens, move out."

Jed watched the Marine step to the shattered window and check the street. He was gone a beat later, outside and out of sight. Jed heard his footsteps crunching through broken glass on the sidewalk.

"Let's go," Maloof said. "You on the SAW, what's your name?"

"Welch. I used to be in the suck before this. Got picked up by Army Civil Affairs."

"It isn't the suck, Marine. It's the Corps. You move out with us."

Bree and the other guys looked like they would try to fight it, but Maloof held himself like an NCO, and gave orders like one. Bree waved at Sharpe, Marks, and Harney to join him by the window. Jed went to stand with Tracy and Pinzler. They followed Maloof out after Bree and the other Army guys left, and not for the first time that day, Jed found himself happy to be back with other Marines.

Maybe this is how it's supposed to be. Only one way to find out, and that's to keep on keepin' on.

Jed let that chant run through his mind as he followed Maloof's team down the street. Up ahead, about twenty meters, Stevens moved through the ruined mess of broken glass and smashed up cars, switching his aim left and right with every step. Jed hefted the SAW and did the same, watching high then low, and praying he wouldn't have to squeeze the trigger again until they were all safe inside somewhere.

194

— 27 —

Meg ran back to the shutters and climbed up to look out the window. Three soldiers were out there, facing off against a single monster in the middle of the street. It skittered back and forth on its claws, like it was trying to keep them penned in. One of them lowered his weapon and flinched, then turned back to look over his shoulder.

The monster on the street flew forward and tackled the man, right in between the other two soldiers. Meg slammed a fist against the steel shutter.

"Who's out there?" Jason said, coming up beside her.

"The Army. Soldiers. I don't know!"

They both watched through the window as the two remaining soldiers killed the monster and the man it had brought down. Then the soldiers moved out of sight, coming across the street and in their direction.

More gunfire crackled from somewhere nearby. Then shouted commands and yelling. One of the soldiers outside ran into the street and was waving at someone. Meg tried to get a look at who he was signaling, but her attention was ripped away by Jason whispering, "Shit. Shit, shit, shit."

A swarm of the monsters poured out of the buildings across the street. Meg's breath caught in her throat as the other soldier she'd seen stepped into the street and started shooting at the monsters. But there were so many.

There's no way he'll hit them all. Those men are going to die.

— 28 —

The fire station was just two blocks up, Maloof had said. Those were the longest two blocks of Jed's life. He could just make out Stevens up at the front, moving in a crouch and darting his muzzle up and down, left and right, as he went. Every few paces, he'd give the signal to hold up while he rushed ahead a bit. Then he'd backpedal and wave them forward.

Every time they stopped, Jed imagined the monsters jumping from the windows to take out the civilians and the LT from before. But nothing came down on top of them. Maloof had put him at the very rear, behind Tracy and Pinzler, so at least he could get away again if he had to.

"Keep that SAW up, Welch. And watch our rear."

At the next corner, Jed spotted the fire station halfway down the block, in between two high rises. The station faced a street that t-boned into the block. A fire truck sat halfway around the corner of the side street; the truck had smashed into the nose of a car there.

Stevens crouched at the near end of the fire truck with

197

Bree and the others just a few meters behind him, all hiding behind a smashed up taxi cab that the truck must have creamed. Maloof, Tracy, and Pinzler held up a little bit behind those guys; they hunkered down around an SUV the fire truck had swiped before it hit the cab. Red paint streaked the taxi and SUV in long lines that looked a lot like blood, only it didn't drip down the side.

Jed sat on his heels with his back against a newspaper stand on the sidewalk. He tried to get a look at Stevens, hoping the guy would move out to the fire station so they could get off this damn street.

"Welch, you watching our ass?" Maloof asked from over his shoulder.

"Yeah," Jed said, turning back to look the way they'd come. He didn't see anything so he went back to eyeballing the back of Steven's helmet, willing the guy to just move the fuck out and bang on the fire station door.

"Welch, last fucking time I'm telling you. Watch our ass."

"Yeah," he said, catching Maloof's eye. "Rah."

Maloof turned away from Jed, shaking his head. He patted the others on the shoulders and they moved up to where Bree and his guys were hiding. Maloof tapped Bree on the back and said something to him. Bree's face pinched up fast, like he was pissed off and about to start swinging, but he went back to that goofy grin of his just as fast. Bree and Maloof said a few more things to each other; their mouths moved but Jed couldn't hear what was being said. Then Bree had his guys come back closer to Jed, near the trashed SUV.

"Yo, Welch."

"Yeah."

"Maloof said to give me the SAW. You go on up and join them. Here," Bree said, handing over his M16. He put it on the ground next to Jed and held his hands out for the SAW.

Jed kept his eye on the fire station door for a beat before unslinging the heavy weapon. Bree almost snatched it out of his hands and whipped the sling over his neck and shoulders in a single motion, like he'd practiced doing it.

Probably was a SAW gunner himself. Dude for sure ain't no fucking corporal.

Jed lifted Bree's rifle and made to move out, but Bree put a hand up.

"Ammo, man. Give it here."

Bree almost had the SAW aiming right at Jed's gut. And his finger was on the trigger.

Jed lifted the ammo pouches off and set them on the ground next to Bree. He knew he'd just fucked himself and the rest of the team, but there was nothing he could do. It wouldn't matter if Jed was infected or not. Bree would light him up if it meant he could get away with the SAW in his hands. The guy was nuts.

"It needs a reload," Jed said, moving off to join the Marines by the taxi cab. When he came up, they were talking over how to approach the fire station.

About time somebody starts thinking. We're fucked if we stay out here.

"Gotta get up there. Signal them to open up," Maloof was saying as Jed came up.

"If they're still in there," Pinzler said.

"Fuck else they gonna be?" Maloof said back, but seemed to rethink the idea a second later. "If they're compromised, we'll shelter in place nearby. The other teams are supposed to rally here at the intersection. We should pop smoke. Stevens, you still got it?"

Stevens shook his head. Then his eyes met Jed's.

"Welch?"

Maloof spun around. "Welch, what—where's the SAW?"

As one, the group of Marines looked back to see Bree and his guys sneaking off the way they'd come. At the corner, Bree turned around and put Harney down with a short burst. Bree and the others were out of sight half a second later.

Jed rammed his elbow into the taxi cab.

"Dammit!"

A scraping sound shook Jed and he looked everywhere to find the source. The door to the fire station was opening. But nobody came out. No Marines to wave them inside, and no firefighters to welcome them in either.

The street was dead silent.

Silent like your daddy's own grave.

His mom used to say that to him. Back when she still wanted him around but didn't want to answer his questions.

You just be silent, Jed.

He wondered why that memory came back to him right now. Of all the things he could think about, why'd he go back to his mom and how much of a bitch she'd been when he was a kid?

The sound of rushing water broke his concentration and he looked at the fire station door again. Water poured out from under the door, but it looked dirty as fuck. Then

Jed realized what he was seeing and nearly threw up.

A flood of bloody water, mixed with bits of who the hell knew what came spilling out from under the door. It was like someone had a fire hydrant turned on in there and was shooting it out into the street the way Jed and Chips used to do with little kids in the summertime.

Only this wasn't the kind of water you'd want to go splashing around in. He could make out body parts, arms and legs, and whole torsos with limbs still on them. Except these weren't human bodies. Some of the monsters must have got inside the station, but if they were being washed out, that meant it was still safe to get inside.

The bodies and blood continued to spill into the street until the flood suddenly stopped. The door didn't go back down right away. Jed wanted to run up there and tell whoever was inside that they were out here.

The crunch of glass under boots came to his ears and Jed snapped his head up. He and the other Marines all scanned left and right. Maloof shuffled forward, around the cab's front bumper.

"What do you see?" Stevens asked.

"Nothing."

Jed had grown pretty damn sick of waiting for dudes with no rank and no sense to tell him what he already knew. And this waiting shit, plus they were down a SAW because of fucking Five-Finger Bree… No, because of Jed's stupid ass letting it go. They were out in the open and under-armed.

"We gotta get inside. Let's go, man."

"We're supposed wait here for the other teams to rally," Pinzler said. "Then we go in."

"Nah, man. Let's go already."

"Keep that attitude under wraps, Marine," Maloof said, coming back from around the cab's bumper. "We were told to hold, we hold."

Jed had it, right there.

Marine? I ain't no fucking Marine.

"This ain't the Corps anymore, man. Look the fuck around you and tell me where you see the Corps. Tell me where you see anything but shit or hell. Man, fuck this."

Jed ignored Maloof's face and the hand he put up. With a grunt, Jed moved out into the street. The fire station door was going back down now. He jogged toward it, but froze after a couple of steps, stopping in the middle of the street. A shriek sliced into the silence around Jed. He spun around to see a monster on top of the fire truck; it was wearing a ripped up ACU and still had boots on. The thing stared down at the other Marines.

Another shriek followed from about a block away, echoing through the urban canyon between the buildings. Jed lifted his rifle, aimed, and squeezed the trigger.

Nothing happened.

That sonofabitch!

Jed backpedaled like mad, dropping the magazine as he moved. Maloof and the others came up and fired at the thing on the truck. It went down, but two more leaped up to take its place. They'd been hiding behind the truck.

Fucking waiting us out. Shit!

Maloof got one of them on the truck, but the other one leaped and scrambled to avoid the Marine's shots. Pinzler pivoted and fired just as Stevens dodged to one side. Pinzler's shot went right into Stevens' back. Jed couldn't move as he watched the Marine go down on his face.

"Fuck! Watch your fire!" Maloof shouted, twisting around Tracy and letting off a burst at the thing just as it jumped from the truck to the top of the taxi cab. Every bullet missed. It flew forward then, launching from the cab in a jump to land behind the Marines, putting it between them and Jed.

"Welch, move it!" Maloof shouted. He, Tracy, and Pinzler held their aim on the thing, but they couldn't fire with Jed standing behind it. The Marines shifted to their left. The monster followed their movement so it was still in between them and Jed.

Things are smart as hell. This is not real. This cannot be real.

Jed shifted left and then right, backing up as he moved, but the monster must have heard him moving, or somehow sensed where he was. It stayed smack between him and the other Marines. Jed was on the sidewalk now, and had fished a new magazine from his pouch. It was his last one.

He could run and hide somewhere.

Jed ditched the thoughts of abandoning the other Marines. He'd do what he could to help them out, but he was still getting inside the fire station whether they came with him or not. He slammed his mag home and charged his weapon. The monster in the street leaped toward the other Marines with its clawed hands out. Tracy's face went white and he dropped his weapon, putting his hands up like he could hide from the monster. It tackled him, putting him on his back right between Maloof and Pinzler.

203

Maloof swung down with a butt stroke to the thing's spine. But it had already started feeding on Tracy. Jed could see the blood and he heard the Marine's screams that quickly turned to gurgling sounds and then silence.

"Fuck!" Maloof shouted, aiming and sending three round bursts into the monster and then Tracy.

Jed had his weapon up, and was aiming in the Marines' direction.

Gotta be ready in case they got infected.

Maloof signaled at Pinzler and they moved toward Jed's position. They seemed fine, and he didn't see any blood on their faces. Jed kept watch down the street, in the direction the fire truck was pointing.

He didn't see any movement. No flashes of white darting behind smashed up cars or into broken storefronts.

A beat later he heard the rattling of a SAW opening up from a block away, then some screams. The SAW cut out quick after that. Then more shouts and the steady cadence of boots on pavement came echoing down the street.

From down the block, at least two squads ran in their direction. Maloof shouted and went into the middle of the street to wave them in.

Jed rocked on his feet, letting the relief flow through him. He even cracked a smile. The scraping sound came again. Jed flashed a look at the fire station door, but it was still shut. Then he realized where the scraping came from. He turned back in time to see Pinzler look up at the building behind the fire truck. The Marine screamed as he opened fire. A swarm of the creatures poured from almost every window on the street.

Jed snapped off shots in every direction he could, trying to keep the monsters from getting to Pinzler. He and Maloof were both covered by the fire truck.

The other squads of Marines came running up the street, taking up positions wherever they could. Two LAWs went streaking at the buildings, blowing concrete and glass everywhere. But that only got two of the monsters. The others leaped clear in time to avoid the blast.

They jumped in time. They saw the fucking LAWs coming in and they jumped.

Jed picked them off if he could, but he mostly tried to stay hidden. He had good cover up top with an awning overhead. If he crouched down, a set of newspaper boxes would block anybody seeing him from the street.

But the monsters would get him if he stayed out here. They'd jump Pinzler and Maloof, then they'd get the others. And then it would just be him, by himself.

Jed shifted right, moving down the sidewalk to the fire station. They'd open the door again. He'd just kick it while he kept an eye on the street. He'd kick it and they'd let him in. Him and anybody fast enough to get in with him.

— 29 —

Meg and Jason had their axes ready. Rachel held the chain in her hands and counted out loud.

"One. Two. Three!"

She yanked down on the chain, hand over hand, until the door was up enough for Meg and Jason to get out. They rushed under it and Meg didn't look back even as she heard the door go down behind them.

The soldiers were going down one by one. They had the monsters kept back with two machine guns taking them out when they appeared in the windows. But then more would come from another window, or from the ground floor of the nearby buildings, and they'd get at least one of the soldiers before the guys with machine guns could move their aim.

"Fuck!" someone yelled to Meg's left. She twisted, ready to swing her axe. A soldier was there with his back against the wall by the station. He had his eyes on the shutters.

Jason got the attention of one of the soldiers in the

street. He moved to join them, so Meg stuck with the guy nearby.

"We gotta get inside!" he yelled at her.

"We will," Meg said, hearing her own voice muffled by her mask. She spoke as clearly as she could to make sure the man could hear and understand. "We have to get the rest of your men."

He nodded, but just kept staring at the shutters and muttering under his breath.

He's in shock. Or scared out of his mind.

Meg thought about banging on the shutters to have Rachel open up for him, but a scream from the street put her mind back on the task.

Save as many as you can, Meg. Nothing's going to slow you down. Not this time.

She left the scared soldier where he was, holding his gun and staring at the shutters.

The monsters had stopped coming out of the windows and were just racing around the street now, like streaks of ghostly white horror in Meg's peripheral vision. She crossed to where Jason and some other soldiers were helping a man who'd been injured.

"Is he infected?" Meg asked as she came up behind them.

"I don't know," Jason said. "I think—"

A gunshot ended the conversation and Meg reeled aside as the injured man's face exploded in a bloody mess. The man who shot him lifted his gun and aimed at a monster charging down the sidewalk toward them. He shot it and then shot another that emerged from the doorway right behind it.

"We have to get them closer to the station, Jason.

They'll die out here."

"I've been trying. They're a little preoccupied!"

The soldiers near them didn't seem ready to hear anything they had to say. They kept their attention on the monsters, shooting, aiming, moving, shooting. Then the whole group moved forward, heading for the fire engine, and another trio came to take their place.

"Please," Meg said to them. "We have to get back inside! You'll get killed out here!"

"Stay down, ma'am," the soldier said. "Out of the line of fire."

He moved away, with the other two men. They followed the first group closer to the engine. That was where the fighting was happening now. Monsters kept leaping onto the truck only to be shot down. But the more monsters the soldiers shot, the more they seemed to ignore what Meg knew was coming.

They're going to run out of ammunition before the city runs out of monsters.

Bullets snapped and zipped around them, and Meg and Jason crouched low as they moved down the street, away from where the fighting was centered. She'd seen more soldiers back that direction. Maybe they would listen and could get the others to retreat into the station.

A final group of five soldiers huddled behind a linen service van that had crashed on its side, blocking the sidewalk. They had a man on his back and were using linens from the van to put a tourniquet on his leg. It was missing below the knee.

"Was he bitten? Did one of them do this?" she asked.

"Grenade," one of them said. "He dropped it."

Jason set his axe down and moved to help the soldiers.

They'd tied the tourniquet, but it hadn't been enough to stop the blood loss.

"I'll get a trauma bag," Meg said, and pivoted to look back down the street to the fire engine. The soldiers seemed to be holding the engine safe from the monsters. They'd lost a lot of men. Only two groups remained that she could see. But they still had the engine as cover, and that meant Meg could get what they needed to help the injured man.

Nothing's going to slow you down, Meg.

She moved out.

***

Jed crouched down against the wall. None of the monsters had seen him yet. They'd stopped coming out of the windows, but he could still hear their screeching and snarling. And the clicking sound of their joints as they moved.

Fuck, fuck, fuck. Gotta get inside.

He shifted to his right, but he'd move out of his covered spot if he got closer to the fire station door. He could sneak out though, just bang on the door and jump back behind cover.

Jed moved to see around the newspaper boxes and came face to face with a monster's puffy lips and yellow eyes that dripped blood down its cheeks. It shrieked at him and he put a bullet into its face. Another one across the street snapped its head up from where it was feeding on a dead Marine. It shifted around and finally spotted him.

Oh shit no. Oh no oh no oh no.

***

Meg came up behind the monster right as it lifted its head and twisted to look at the soldier hiding by the station. With a grunt, Meg put her axe into the monster's head, nearly taking if off at the neck. Another one sprang down from above and landed in front of her, hissing and smacking its puffy sucker lips together.

Her axe was still stuck in the first one, and she felt her guts almost let go as the second monster jumped toward her. It jerked to the side in mid-air and fell flat on the pavement at her feet.

Meg staggered back and yanked her axe free. The soldier on the sidewalk by the station waved at her, and then he dropped down out of sight again.

Fine. He's hiding, but he's helping at least. Not like Rex.

Double-checking the windows above her for movement, Meg moved down the street, keeping her eyes on the trauma gear spilling out of the engine up ahead. Three soldiers leaned up against the truck, firing into windows in the buildings on both sides of the street. One man with a machine gun kept back a few feet and aimed over their heads at anything that leaped up onto the engine.

Four men. Is that all that's left?

The bodies around the street confirmed her worst fear. They'd already failed to save most of the soldiers. And some of the bodies had begun to shudder as the infection spread into the injured men who hadn't died yet. Meg crouched and moved forward, aiming at the trauma bag she spotted on the ground next to the engine. She came up beside one of the soldiers.

"Ma'am, you need to get out of here," he said.

"I'm here to help."

"With what?" he said, still shooting.

"Changing!" another man near the truck yelled. Meg twisted her head to look over her shoulder. The man was reloading. The monsters were coming slower now. Only a few appeared in the windows and were quickly shot down.

Or they're sneaking back to hide inside, hoping these guys will run out of ammo.

The thought scared her. The monsters had shown they could still think. But could they really plan like that?

"You're going to run out of ammo if you don't get inside!" she yelled, hoping they all heard her. "And some of these bodies are going to turn. Go to the fire house. We have someone inside to let you in."

Meg grabbed up the trauma bag by her feet and raced away from the engine. She sprinted down the street to where the others were hiding by the linen van. Half way to their position she stopped running and dropped the trauma bag.

Oh, God. Where are they? Where's Jason?

All Meg could see were bloodied bodies and monsters feeding on them.

"Hel— *Help!*" Meg screamed, backpedaling for all she was worth.

***

Jed watched the lady firefighter grab the medic kit and run away from the firetruck. She crouched down and ran like hell, like she'd been in combat or something. She knew how to move, or wasn't afraid to try at least.

He was glad he could save her back there when the thing was about to jump her. Fucking monsters were taking them all down. Only half a squad was left, and the guy with the M27 in the street, he was about to get it if he didn't find some cover soon.

Jed popped two rounds at a creature trying to crawl around the side of the fire truck. The guys there didn't even notice, just kept shooting every time one of the monsters came into view.

"Y'all fall back! You gotta fall back!" Jed shouted. If they heard him, they didn't show it.

Fine. Fuck it. I gave you the call.

Jed looked for the firefighter lady again. She was headed down the street, back the way she'd come from. A second later, she dropped the medic kit and screamed.

Jed moved out of hiding and lifted his weapon. He heard another scream from behind him and pivoted to watch the guy with the M27 go down under two of the monsters. Their claws raked into him and he roared as he tried to fight them off. But it was no use. They ripped into him while he thrashed. Jed had his weapon on them, but the firefighter lady was screaming for help down the street. Jed spun in her direction and saw her running backwards. She whipped around, half stumbling up the street and aiming for his position. She got her feet under her and ran full tilt, waving her axe in the air.

"Inside! Inside!" she yelled. Her mask muffled her voice, but not so much that Jed couldn't hear what she was saying.

He dodged to the side and aimed in her direction.

Four of the monsters charged up the street behind her like a pack of wild dogs. He knew he should shoot them, but a heavy fear held his finger away from the trigger.

What if he missed them? What if he hit her?

But he had to shoot now. If he didn't, then this was it for Jed Welch.

"Now or never, Jed. Now or fucking never," he said to himself as he forced his finger around the trigger.

He squeezed off a shot and put the first monster down with a hole in its face. He did the others just the same. One, two, and three.

The guys from near the fire truck ran over beside him right as the lady firefighter came up. The monsters were still out there. Their shrieking and scraping claws seemed to echo off of every wall. Broken glass tinkled and cracked somewhere nearby.

"We gotta go," one of the other guys said.

"We're US Marines, ma'am," Jed said to the lady firefighter. She looked around the street like she was stunned.

"Ma'am," Jed said again. "We gotta get inside. You got people in there, right? People can let us in?"

"Yeah," she said.

They moved back toward the fire station door. Jed kept his weapon up. The other guys had theirs up, but one guy only held it ready, not up and aimed out.

"Eyes out, man," Jed told him and motioned with his weapon for the other guy to bring his muzzle up.

"I'm out, man. Got no ammo."

"Shit. Guys over there still have it on them. They didn't even get a shot off, right?"

"They're covered in blood," the lady firefighter said.

214

"You can't touch them. You aren't wearing gloves."

Jed looked at her. She had her axe in both hands and stood ready, like she'd move out into the street. One of the other guys, the one who still had ammo, came up next to her. He dropped his mag and handed it to this buddy, then popped his ammo pouch open and took out his last one.

"I'll cover you. C'mon."

She nodded at the guy and they stepped off together, aiming for the first bunch of bodies right across the street.

"Get what's in their weapons," Jed yelled after them. The guy next to him slotted the half-empty mag into his weapon and charged it.

A shriek put them all on alert and Jed whipped his weapon up and around the street, looking for whatever made the noise. He couldn't see it, though, just busted out windows, blood everywhere, and bodies on the ground.

The guy next to him opened up, firing over their heads. Jed spun around. Three of the things were crawling down the wall of the fire station right at them.

— 30 —

"Run!" Meg yelled, shoving a hand against the Marine's shoulder. "Back to the station!" He stumbled away for a step, then lifted his rifle and started shooting.

"No!" Meg yelled, but it was already too late. Three of the monsters jumped away from the building and landed in the street, surrounding the young man. He spun to one side and fired, but he missed the monster. Before he could shoot again, the other two tackled him and ripped into his body with their clawed hands.

Meg charged with her axe up and swung at the one nearest her. She sliced the top of its head off and followed her swing around as she jumped over the dead man at her feet. She landed facing off against the remaining two monsters with her axe at the ready. The nearest monster reared up and the one behind it began circling around Meg to the right.

It went down with a bullet hole in its chest, and the one nearest to her flinched, backing up a step and looking around her shoulder.

It knows. It can tell where the threat is coming from.

217

"Get inside!" Meg yelled as she stepped backwards, keeping her axe up to guard against the thing in front of her. It's puffy mouth popped and smacked in a sickening rhythm that turned Meg's stomach. She swallowed against the urge to vomit and focused on the weight of the axe in her hands. She'd have to time it right, but she'd kill the monster and then they'd get inside.

The monster leaped away, to the side, and then raced forward and leaped again. Meg turned in time to see another of the Marines taken down in a snarling mess of blood and tearing claws.

The Marine who had been hiding fired at both of them, the monster and the man it tackled. Meg rushed forward as two more of the monsters dropped down beside the shutters, penning them in.

***

Jed slammed his boot heel into the steel shutter door behind him. The lady firefighter had her axe up, and he had his rifle at the ready for a butt stroke.

Goddamned bone dry magazine. We're gonna die.

The door creaked behind him, but it didn't move. The monsters kept circling him and the lady firefighter, sometimes lifting their heads and sniffing. The one in front of him bit its own hand and chewed out a bunch of muscle and blood. It puckered its mouth.

"Oh hell. Oh hell oh hell oh hell," Jed said.

The lady firefighter got in front of him and Jed instantly spun around to make sure the other one didn't get him from behind. But it was on the ground with a deep cut down the middle of its face.

"You—You saved me," he said, backing up against the shutter and banging on it with his foot. The lady firefighter kept dancing with the one in the street. It tried to get around her and she put her axe up. Then it skittered the other way and she spun to match it, step for damn step.

"Keep banging on the door," she said.

Jed did what she said, slamming his heel into the door again and again. He only stopped when he saw the faces in every window in the building across the street.

***

Meg darted forward with her axe, trying to feint at the thing to get it to commit. She'd learned a little about how they moved in just the last few minutes. Wherever they saw a threat, they'd go for it. As long as she looked more threatening than the man behind her, she could save him. And she was confidant she could take the monster out this time.

She'd lost count of how many she'd killed so far, but her axe dripped with their blood, and before she went down it would drip with more.

The creak and groan of metal sounded from behind her. Meg heard the chain rattling as Rachel cracked the shutters open.

"Get in," Meg said to the Marine at her back. The one in front of her was still staring at her, and slowly shifting on its feet. Left to right. Left to right, staring at her and shifting its position. Left to—

"Shit!" Meg yelled. More of them were creeping down the wall of the building across the street. In the instant

AJ SIKES

that she took her eyes off the one near her, it jumped, and she just had the strength to put her axe up to block it from tackling her.

It rebounded and launched again from the sidewalk to her right. The man behind her ran forward and swung his gun around to hit it in the side of the head with the stock. She heard a loud crack, and then shrieks as the ones on the wall began dropping and charging for them.

***

Jed finished the thing off with a second butt stroke, making sure its head was caved in on one side before he darted backwards and dropped down to roll under the fire station door.

The lady firefighter was already on the ground doing the same thing when Jed got inside. A mass of arms and legs raced for them from across the street, and the snarls and shrieks were like knives in his ears, pushing him to get inside as fast as he could.

"Close it!" someone near him yelled. Jed got his knees under him and lifted up from the floor in time to see a different firefighter grabbing at a chain that worked the door. It was another woman, with dark hair hanging out from around her mask.

Then she was falling, slamming onto the floor. Her head bounced off the concrete and a stain of blood marked where she hit. It smeared as her body was yanked out of the fire station.

She didn't even get to scream.

***

Meg threw herself toward the clawed hands reaching in, with her axe held out. But they were too fast. Claws wrapped around Rachel's ankles and tore her legs out from under her. A sickening crack filled Meg's ears and then Rachel was gone, ripped from the room right in front of her eyes.

The Marine was there, reaching for the chain to close the door, but he was too far back from it. He leaned over the spot where Rachel had been, trying to catch the chain with his gun and pull it closer to him.

Meg lunged for the chain and in two quick movements had the door closed. She fell against the wall and slumped. Her axe clattered on the floor beside her, and Meg shook and then roared with sorrow.

***

"Thank you for helping me," Jed said. They were the only words he could think to say. The only words that made any sense any more. Everything else in Jed's mind was a mess. Even the lady firefighter was a mess, shaking and crying. He could see tears flowing out of her eyes behind her mask.

"Why didn't you shoot it?" she asked. She didn't look at him, just stared at the ground between her boots while she sobbed.

"My—No ammo. I got nothing left."

They stayed like that for a few beats while the monsters clawed and shrieked outside the door. The lady firefighter looked at the chain a few times, and Jed figured maybe she was thinking just to open it up. Let the fuckers in and that'd be that.

Gotta get her back on her feet. What the fuck do you say, man? What do you—

"What's—What's your name, ma'am?"

"I'm Meg Pratt," she said, cutting into his thoughts. "You're…?"

"My name's… I'm Private Welch, but you can call me Jed. I'm Jed."

***

Meg caught that he mumbled the word *private*, but gave her his first name with more force. Something was off about him. He was different from the soldiers out on the street. The ones she couldn't save. Or maybe he'd just survived the worst battle imaginable and was in shock. He had said he was a private after all, so this could have been the first time he'd ever seen war.

Not like Meg had seen it before herself, but she'd been through plenty that was just as bad.

Maybe as bad as regular war. The kind where people just shoot each other or blow each other up. Nothing like this, though. Nothing at all.

"We had some more survivors with us," Meg said. "They got in, though. The monsters."

They'd stopped shrieking outside and she only heard a few of them moving around. Their claws scraped on the door sometimes, but it seemed like they'd given up.

For now, maybe. They'll be back. They always come back.

"You're the only one left, ma'am?" the Marine asked. Meg had to smile. He had a southern accent, and the way he said *ma'am* sounded so polite. Such a difference to everything else around her.

"Yeah. Me, you, and Rex."

"Rex? He the fire dog or something?"

Meg let out a sharp laugh as she looked at the stairs. Rex was on the steps with one hand on the wall and his axe clutched against his chest with the other hand. He had a dopey-dog look on his face, like something Meg had seen in a Norman Rockwell painting. "Yes, Jed. That's exactly who Rex is."

She picked up her axe and struggled to her feet. Meg nodded at Rex, indicating Jed with her axe.

"He's a Marine. He's out of ammo, but he's okay."

Rex seemed to relax a bit. He came down to the app floor and approached them cautiously.

"You—You weren't infected, right?" he asked the Marine.

Jed shook his head, but didn't say anything.

"We should set up guard duty," Meg said. "Get some rest. Sleep if we can."

Jed nodded and mumbled that he'd take the first shift.

— 31 —

April 20th, 2015
Upper East Side, Manhattan

When she woke up to Jed shaking her shoulder, Meg had no idea what time it was. But it didn't feel like she'd had much sleep. She got up anyway, picked up her axe and went to stand at the top of the stairs. From there she could see through the windows in the dorm room in case anything tried to get in.

They'd nailed more boards up to make a tighter grid, and reinforced the others that Rex had nailed back after the things broke in earlier.

They'll hold. And if they don't, then it's just time to accept it I guess.

Her two hour shift passed in silence, except for the grisly sounds of the monsters on the street outside. Meg was supposed to wake Rex up for the last guard shift, but she couldn't sleep anyway, so she stayed up for the rest of the night.

Daylight finally broke and she went to the dorm room

windows to watch the street. Streams of the infected moved like trails of giant ants as they slinked away from the morning light coming into the ruined street, illuminating the bodies and the blood of the night before. A few monsters picked at the bodies, but quickly moved away, like they would rather ignore the dead.

Don't want a cold dinner, huh?

Meg looked at Jed and Rex sleeping in their bunks. Jed lay still with his empty weapon beside him. Rex held an axe by the handle, but the head hung down beside his bunk.

She'd done it. Finally, after all the blood and the hell and the agony of watching people die all around her, Meg had saved two people.

A man with an empty gun and another man with only half a spine, if that.

"Maybe there's a yellow brick road somewhere in this city," Meg said to herself. "We'll find the wizard and get them what they need."

She laughed, a sad and hollow sound inside the near silence of the dorm room. Rex snored softly behind her and Jed mumbled something in his sleep.

It would have been so easy, so many times, to just join Tim in death. To let the monsters get to her, or to just take herself out. She had no shortage of opportunities to die or just kill herself over the past twenty-four hours. But she hadn't taken any of them.

As she watched the monsters crawl away into the shadows outside, the thought that she may have been better off dead kept nagging at her, like a hangnail rubbing against her other fingers.

"No," she said, eyeing the last of the monsters on the street. "You don't get to win. Not today. And maybe not ever."

END OF BOOK ONE.

The story continues in

PENANCE

book 2 of the Redemption trilogy

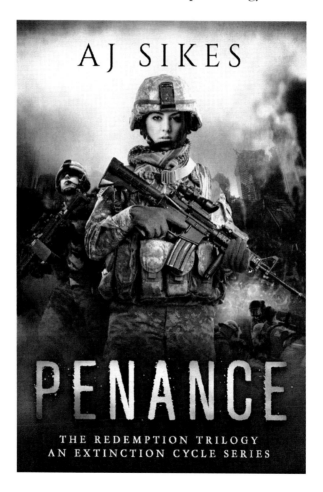

Available at Amazon Books

About the Author, AJ Sikes

AJ Sikes is a freelance editor and author. His short stories have been published by Fox Spirit Books and Hamilton Springs Press. Sikes is a US Army veteran, father, and woodworker. If he's not at his desk, he's in his shop. Or possibly dealing with whatever the children or cats have gotten into.

Follow him on Twitter @AJSikes_Author
Join his spam free mailing list here: AJSikes.com

About the Author, Nicholas Sansbury Smith

Nicholas Sansbury Smith is the New York Times and USA Today bestselling author of the Hell Divers series. His other work includes the Extinction Cycle series, the Trackers series, and the Orbs series. He worked for Iowa Homeland Security and Emergency Management in disaster planning and mitigation before switching careers to focus on his one true passion—writing. When he isn't writing or daydreaming about the apocalypse, he enjoys running, biking, spending time with his family, and traveling the world. He is an Ironman triathlete and lives in Iowa with his wife, their dogs, and a house full of books.

Are you a Nicholas Sansbury Smith fan?
Join him on social media.
He would love to hear from you!

Facebook Fan Club: Join the NSS army!
Facebook Author Page: **Nicholas Sansbury Smith**
Twitter: @GreatWaveInk
Website: NicholasSansburySmith.com
Instagram: instagram.com/author_sansbury
Email: Greatwaveink@gmail.com

Manufactured by Amazon.ca
Acheson, AB

12306182R00136